Oracle in the Mist

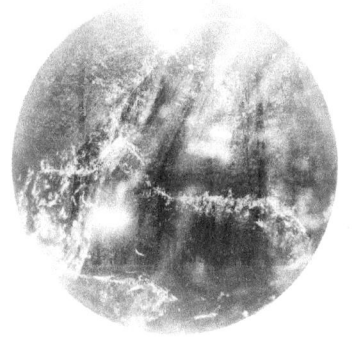

LINDA MAREE MALCOLM

Oracle in the Mist
Linda Maree Malcolm

Published by JoJo Publishing
First published 2012
'Yarra's Edge'
2203/80 Lorimer Street
Docklands VIC 3008 Australia
Email: jo-media@bigpond.net.au or visit
www.jojopublishing.com

JoJo Publishing
Designer / typesetter: Working Type Studio (www.workingtype.com.au)
Edited by Ormé Harris

National Library of Australia Cataloguing-in-Publication entry
Author: Malcolm, Linda Maree.
Title: Oracle in the mist / Linda Maree Malcolm.
ISBN: 9780987192769 (pbk.)
Subjects: Detective and mystery stories.
                 Magic--Fiction.
Dewey Number: A823.4

Acknowledgements

My gratitude to my husband Sandro for generously recognising my needs and providing me with all of the tools and enthusiasm and encouragement that were necessary for my development as a writer and to my children and grandchild, for motivating me to write and for being the inspiration for my characters. My beautiful Italian family opened up my mind, accepting and supporting me with love and taught me about their culture. They provided the safety net to my tightrope and always will.

When I became too serious, my wonderful homeschool community, especially the lovely Melissa, Paula, Rachel, Lisa and Lee, were there for me with their strength, understanding and fun.

Thank you to my mother Doreen, who also loved to write, for teaching me that to follow a dream is a very sacred thing. My father, Stan, and my brothers and sisters and their children have always encouraged and believed in me. Memories of my two late grandmothers inspired some ideas used in the book. Bobby is named for my paternal grandmother.

I would like to acknowledge my writing teacher, the late Jenni Overend – an angel in life and in the hereafter and also my Year Nine English teacher, Mrs Harris for telling me I had a talent for writing.

My professional friends, Marisa, Frank, Lou, Barry, Jo, Duncan and Katie and all of my other friends and family members have been very supportive. Thank you.

My gratitude to the psychics and mediums and all of the people who have taught and guided me over the years and to my Spiritual Advisor, who has been with me for every step of this journey.

Dedication

For my family, Sandro, Thomas, Amy, Zac, Madeline, Reuben and Isabella.

I continue to be amazed and inspired by their poetic, musical, artistic and writing abilities and feel blessed to be a part of this group.

I hope that we will always be united by our desire to live mainly in our imaginations.

About the author

Linda Maree Malcolm worked at a wide variety of jobs before deciding in 2008 to make writing her main focus. The homeschooling mother of four has been completely absorbed in a world of imagination as she has read aloud hundreds of books to her children.

She was raised in the Dandenong Mountains and then moved to the beautiful Yarra Valley where, as a single mother of one, she married her husband, whose heritage is Italian. Linda has a deep understanding of the esoteric world.

Linda has drawn on some of her own experiences when writing this book, loosely basing the characters of *Oracle in the Mist* on people she has met via homeschooling as well as on her own children, but her main inspiration comes from Beatrix Potter, Enid Blyton, JRR Tolkien, CS Lewis and LM Montgomery.

Contents

Chapter 1
THE DANCE OF THE FAIRIES

I ntuition told Bobby that she should wake up as there was something going on that she should know about. She sat up in her bed and listened — yes there it was, beautiful music that seemed a great distance away. Who would be playing music at this time of the night? Certainly not her mother who was probably asleep in her own bedroom, just down the hall.

Bobby did not feel frightened as she threw back her quilt to go and investigate. It was extreme curiosity that drove her and as she tiptoed down the hall she noticed that the music was becoming louder:

"We come, softly through the night, as evening falls behind us. Our footsteps leave no mark upon the snow.

Let your spirit go it will find us."

Bobby descended the stairs and walked into the kitchen, listening for the melodious singing again. It had become far away again and she realised that she had somehow taken the wrong direction:

"We come adorned in spider web and dew, through woodland to the meadow. We come luminous and bright, dancing with the light and the shadow.

"The summer moon is calling us to play, a sacred light to guide us. The wild music leads us in a trance, spinning to the dances inside us."

Bobby climbed the stairs again and holding onto the old banister looked around her. This didn't make any sense. She could hear the singing, it was all around her and yet it seemed to be coming from nowhere. She went to the bathroom and noticed that the sounds became closer:

"The air is warm and echoes with the sound of laughter rising higher.

With drums and bells we sing into the night dancing in the light of the fire."

She looked above her and the realisation dawned on her. It wasn't in her home at all. Or at least not on this level or the one below. It was in the attic. It had to be — there was no other explanation. Bobby suddenly remembered that there was a pull-down ladder from the attic in the walk-in linen press which was located right next to the bathroom. She tiptoed quietly into that room so as not to wake her mother and, without turning on the light, felt about above her for the string that would pull the attic ladder down. There it was. She gave it a gentle tug but it didn't move. It was quite stuck and the thought occurred to Bobby that it had not been used in some time. She ignored her logical side asking the question, how did whoever is in the attic get in? This was no time for logic.

She used all of her strength to pull at the string and just when she thought it would never budge, it came open, just a crack at first pouring years of dust and goodness knows what else onto her upturned face and into her eyes, nose and open mouth. While she brushed and wiped at herself Bobby became aware of two things. The light that now emanated from the crack in the ceiling was almost as bright if not brighter than ordinary daylight. The singing and music was very close now and she had been correct in her assumption that it was from the attic:

"We weave a music curiously pure, a crystal song suspended.

We fly on wings diaphanous as light, dancing till the long night is ended."

Even if Bobby was afraid, which she wasn't, to see what was above her, there was no way she could resist the magnetic pull of the music. She had become completely entranced by it. The leading voice was the richest and purest she had ever heard.

"We come, ancient as the moon, as new as every season.

We come as fire as icicle and leaf; suspend your disbelief and your reason."

Bobby pulled at the ladder which became straightened out in one smooth action. Quietly climbing the rickety stairs she took a deep breath to prepare herself for what she might see above her. As her head entered the blinding light emanating from the attic, Bobby squinted to adjust her vision. She gripped the top rung tightly and just in time too because what she saw took her breath away to the point of making her almost topple back down the ladder. In the centre of the enormous attic was what at first glance seemed to be a massive bonfire that stretched at least three metres high. So this was what was creating the light in the room.

But even more astonishing than that was what Bobby saw either dancing or relaxing around the light. It was impossible; it couldn't be true! Dozens of tiny

Linda Maree Malcolm

incandescent beings, all with long lustrous hair and floating garments, some with wings and some without but nevertheless all flying about and also frequently stopping to dance with one another; a dance that was simple enough but seemed to somehow have them all laughing in unison. Their laughter was the loveliest of sounds and right then and there Bobby decided that a sound such as that could only come from fairy creatures, of which she had read but never before actually seen.

Then another sight leapt before her eyes. On the floor were many other types of beings that Bobby supposed would be referred to as elves, all with long pointed ears. There were also leprechauns, pixies and brownies. Some were playing instruments, some were dancing. Others were making shoes with tiny steel hammers and still others were talking with one another or singing or simply watching and laughing to themselves. But the grandest of all of the creatures were the tall forest elves. Clothed in only leaves and twigs sewn together and with golden hair streaming down their backs and reaching to their knees, these elves were involved in a more formal kind of dance. Half of them male and half female, they held hands with one another in a circle around the fire. Then the men would drop their left hands and the women their right hands and the men would lead the women under their arms. Then, holding their joined hands to their faces would step in a most dramatic fashion, circling around each other. They would then swap hands and circle the fire and every so often drop hands and then change partners. The men would give a slight bow and the women a little curtsy.

It was only now that Bobby noticed that these elven creatures were so unreal as to be almost transparent and indeed she suddenly realised that each of them was completely hollow in the back, just like a hollowed out tree. Another character caught her eye. He was very small, only about one and a half metres tall and had curly ginger hair with a matching beard. He wore green clothes that were quite ragged and on his head he wore a red cap. He looked half-starved and overworked and he stared at Bobby and then smiled at her and gestured for her to come into the circle. Bobby thought it odd that he was the only one that had noticed her so far. Would the others notice her if she stepped forward? She walked toward the fire, feeling quite magical and mythical also, her long white cotton and lace nightgown billowing out behind her. She thought she would like to dance and sing as well and wondered if she were under some kind of enchantment. All thoughts of the real world, her mother and moving house, had completely vanished from her mind. Right then all of the singing, dancing and flying about came to an abrupt halt. It was replaced with screams of terror and with the blink of an eye the whole party had vanished, a long thin stream of light exiting through the window.

Linda Maree Malcolm

"Don't go, please come back. I won't hurt you!" Bobby called out but it was too late and before she knew it she found herself in the middle of an ancient and massive attic, all alone except for the forgotten furniture and piles of dust. Bobby awoke with a start. She sat up in bed and noticed that she was pulling at her own collar. She stared around her to try and get her bearings. Yes, that's right — new room, new house, new town. But there was something else on the edge of her memory; what was it …

Oh yes, she remembered now, a magical place full of beautiful music and strange elemental creatures. But where was it? She tried to remember for a moment but then heard her mother calling her name from down the hall. It was just a dream, anyway, she thought to herself. And dreams usually meant nothing at all.

She bounced out of bed feeling quite light and excited, although she had no idea why. She bounded into the kitchen to greet her mother and they chatted away about what was coming up for them for the day. Her mother asked her to get a tablecloth that was kept in the linen press. As soon as Bobby opened the door of the walk-in cupboard she remembered her dream from the previous night.

A fairy dance in her attic, that's right. She looked up and sure enough there was the string to pull the ladder down just like in her dream. But it was only a dream, she told herself. Stuff like that did not happen in real life, did it? Still, she thought to herself, later, when her mother was doing the reading for a client she would come back to the linen press, pull down the ladder and explore the attic.

Chapter 2

THE CRYSTAL BALL AND THE ORACLE

B obby pulled the ladder down easily enough and was relieved that there was no dust emptied onto her face. Before she knew it she was standing in the exact same spot as in her dream looking at the exact same attic full of knick knacks and old furniture. The only difference was that in the centre of the room, rather than there being a bonfire, there was a pillar of concrete with a length of red fabric draped over it. She was disappointed to say the least. She had hoped to find some hint of what she thought she had seen here last night. Still, this was a good opportunity to explore her new house. She longed to find some clue as to the life of her grandmother, who had lived here before her for decades.

All she'd noticed so far was cobwebs, dust and mouse droppings. Bobby's grandmother had been a woman of mystery; she lived like a hermit, rarely venturing out and Bobby had only met her a couple of times in her life. The last time Bobby had seen her was six years earlier. Bobby remembered that she still had those eyes that seemed so full of sorrow, as if they were the keepers of some terrible secret. But her grandmother was such a warm and loving person who talked easily to people and made them feel at home by getting them laughing at all kinds of things, usually her own shortcomings. Her ability to make you feel at ease almost made you forget the fact that she seemed on the verge of tears a lot of the time.

Now that Bobby was twelve she was getting curious about the people in her family. She couldn't help feeling that there were a lot of secrets being kept from her and she now realised that all adults were very good at keeping things from children. They did it out of love of course; they didn't want their children to experience too much too soon for fear that it would make them grow up before their time. Bobby had worked this out by watching her own mother, Daphne. Whenever a client came for Daphne to give an angel card reading, Bobby had to be completely out of ear shot. Bobby understood that the client's privacy had to be protected too but there was also a feeling of protecting Bobby from knowing all of the things that happened to adults and Bobby could never quite figure out what those things were.

It was frustrating and she repeatedly told Daphne to stop treating her like a little girl but Daphne only answered her questions to a point which left Bobby to find out the rest by herself. If she could only find some sort of clue as to her grandmother's life here in the attic, she might come closer to knowing what kind of person

Linda Maree Malcolm

her grandmother was and why the fairies had led her here in the first place.

There was an assortment of floral boxes stacked one on top of the other in the corner of the attic. Bobby looked through each one but found nothing except bits of old fabric, buttons, cottons and dressmaking patterns. Next to the boxes was an antique dresser but the drawers were empty. She was about to leave the attic but something made her walk towards the pillar in the centre of the room. She pulled the red fabric off it and there sitting on the pillar was a large crystal ball. She knew it was a crystal ball because one of her mother's friends was a clairvoyant who used a crystal ball to tell the future. This one was different though because on it were written the words "Oracle in the Mist" in very fancy gold print.

It really was the largest and most important looking crystal ball she'd ever seen. Underneath the crystal ball were three newspaper articles that were quite ancient and that had been taped together with sticky tape that was now yellowed and curled and that had almost lost its ability to stick. Bobby gently eased the newspaper out from under the crystal ball. Something told her this was not a ball she would want to break.

She replaced the ball and unfolded the newspaper. She saw that the largest article was dated 19th November, 1930. There was a picture of eight children all dressed in old-fashioned clothes such as overalls and long-waisted dresses. The girls' hair was cut into short bobs and the boys had bowl cuts.

The headline read: "A miracle. Eight children missing for six days return home safely." The article went on to explain that the parents and police still had no clue as to where the children had been because the children had no memory whatsoever of the incident. Apparently the parents just woke up one day to find their children at home and sleeping in their beds again, much to their utter relief but also shock.

Bobby noticed the newspaper was called *Queensborough Times* which confirmed that this had happened right here in this little country town. She looked at the names of the children pictured and recognised her own grandmother's name, Robina Fairweather.

She studied the picture. Her grandmother appeared to be staring at the gap next to her as if wondering at the absence of someone. And there were those huge sad eyes, thought Bobby, even in this picture when her grandmother was only a child. The article said that the children all told exactly the same story; they had no idea where they had been but were happy to be home and eager to be getting on with their lives.

Bobby read the next article: "Locals talk of alien craft sighting on night of 19th November, 1930." The next article after that read: "Mr and Mrs Game have finally become proud parents after adopting a bonny, black-haired baby boy." Bobby folded the newspaper and put it into her jean pocket. Instinct told her she would be referring to it again. She read the words on the ball out loud to herself: "Oracle in the Mist." What does it mean, she thought to herself? And why has it been left up here with these articles for so long. She picked up the ball and held it in front of her face.

Right at that moment the most peculiar thing started to happen. Tiny white mists began to swirl around inside the ball. She desperately wanted to put the ball back but she was frozen to the spot. Her heart began to pound almost audibly. What was happening? Time seemed to stand still and all she was able to do was stare into the ball. But then she had real reason to be afraid because the ball started to pulsate and the mists exited the ball and flew around in circles, becoming larger and stronger until they were swirling around the room, whipping up her hair. Bobby heard her name being called, quietly at first and then much louder and with urgency. This can't be happening, she thought.

The ball then screamed her name making her jump and she almost dropped the ball. She began to feel incredibly dizzy and wondered if this was how you felt right before you fainted. And then the voice came loud and clear, cutting through the confusion and fear. "Bobby, I've been calling you for ages, where are you?"

It was Daphne calling up the attic stairs. At that moment the mists stopped swirling and re-entered the ball. It stopped pulsating and became a normal crystal ball again. Bobby calmed herself enough to replace the ball on the pedestal. At that moment Bobby heard the client's car driving out of their driveway and realised that the angel card client was leaving. She ran toward the attic stairs and glancing back at the ball wondered if what she had just seen had really happened at all. What was it all about and did it have anything to do with the happenings of the night before?

"Yes, I heard you, I'm coming," she answered her mother. That's right, it was time to go to the home-school group meeting, she remembered. As she hurried down the attic ladder her fear was replaced with something else. She couldn't help feeling excited. Something told her she was on the verge of an incredible adventure.

Chapter 3

SHARING FAMILY SECRETS

B obby hopped into the car to go to the home-schoolers' meeting at the library with Daphne. She hadn't been looking forward to going, even after Daphne had told her that it would be good to get out and meet other home-schoolers. But at least now she had something to do when she got there. She would look for books relating to the town's history which would hopefully lead to more information about her grandmother's life. She was bursting to tell someone about what she had found in the attic and was about to mention it to Daphne but then thought better of it. Her mother was very open-minded but somehow Bobby couldn't imagine Daphne allowing her keep the ball once she knew what it was capable of. No, she would just have to keep it to herself for now. One thing was for sure — these two items were linked somehow. She was determined to find out how the newspaper article related to the crystal ball.

She headed toward the historical section of the library where there was a book on display called "The history of our beautiful town, Queensborough". She flicked back to 1930 and sure enough there was a page with the heading: "Enormous oak on the Brewsters' property that the alien craft sighting took place at".

She looked at the picture. It really was the biggest oak tree she had ever seen. There was also a story about how a local man witnessed several lights and what seemed like lightning strikes hovering above the tree late one spring night. Bobby took out the newspaper articles to compare the dates. They matched exactly.

"Pretty amazing tree," someone said from behind her. She snapped the book closed, stuffed the article back into her pocket and spun around all at the same time. There before her stood a boy, about her own age, with thick, curly black hair, a perfect face and very sensible clothes. She didn't answer him. She couldn't actually and she wasn't sure why. It was as if her tongue had been bitten by bees and was caught way back in her throat. It was usually Bobby who talked easily to strangers and could think of a clever thing to say on just about every subject and so she wondered at her own speechlessness. The more she noticed it, the more a blush began to creep up her face. Her lily white, freckled skin was turning a deep crimson red and she could feel her red, woolly hair standing up on end. Luckily for her, the boy must have sensed her unease and took the lead by introducing himself.

"David Game, at your service," he said and bowed very

low, crossing his arms in front of himself and dipping his head, in the most dramatic way. Now Bobby giggled and went to introduce herself. "Oomph" was what came out of her mouth instead of normal words. Being even more embarrassed now than before, she turned to put the book back on to the shelf, hoping he wouldn't mistake her shyness for extreme rudeness. Luckily for her he wasn't offended by her tongue tie at all. You see, he had been very well brought up and so proceeded to make conversation with her in a plain, matter-of-fact fashion.

"I hope you don't think I creep up on people like that all the time but I couldn't help noticing that you're looking at my favourite book. I love that old oak out on the Brewsters' property. It really is the most amazing tree and I guess it caught my attention because I also have a personal interest in it. My grandfather had a funny story to tell about that tree and I often go and just look at it. I have to tell you it really is the most remarkable and beautiful tree I have ever seen. You could live your whole life under it, sleep under it, work under it, celebrate under it and still not tire of it. That is how marvellous it is. It's been a tourist attraction for some years now ..."

"Really," Bobby heard herself say and was relieved to have her voice back. She wondered at this boy's ability to talk so fast without even taking a breath. Was this the real him or was he just showing off?

He drew a deep breath and then started again. "Oh

yes," he continued, "people come from all over Australia and all over the world in fact, just to look at it and sit under it. It's a very special tree with a special kind of energy and it seems to want to tell you a story although I don't know that anyone has ever actually heard it talk." He paused to look at her. "Of course …" and he would have continued had she not spoken quite loudly over the top of him.

"Well, that sounds fascinating," she said, glad that her confidence had returned and trying not to sound too sarcastic. She looked at the boy straight in the eye.

"Thank you for that information. And now I'm going that way," she said, pointing toward the Teenager section. Would he take the hint on hearing her fake politeness? It was becoming clear to her that she would have to bring this conversation to an end or he would just keep babbling on until they turned grey or to stone or whatever came first.

"It's not just the tree but the events that took place around the tree that I find most interesting," he said and took a step in front of her to block her exit. How dare he do that, she thought to herself. Who did he think he was? She didn't want to get to know him more and she certainly didn't want to be sharing information with him about the tree or anything else for that matter. And he couldn't force her either. She'd never met anyone so … so … boyish; yes that's what it was. Her girlfriends would never behave this way. He stared into her eyes as if that would somehow hypnotise her but it only made her more determined to get away from him. Every time she took a step to the right or the left he would take the same step to block her. All the while she was fiddling with the article in her pocket. Clearly he was hoping to get some information from her. Her logic told her it would be silly to share her secret with someone she had just met but there was something about his eyes that seemed almost familiar, somehow. Still, she wasn't used to anyone being in her personal space like this and she found it very annoying. They stood looking at one another.

"What do you want?" she finally asked.

The strange boy replied, "I'd like to get to know you more, if that's okay. After all, isn't that what homeschool group is about — meeting new people, making new friends? There's nothing wrong with that, is there?"

Bobby thought he sounded sincere enough but his eyes gave him away. He kept glancing at the jeans pocket that held the newspaper article that she was fiddling with.

"No, but I've got somewhere else I need to be," Bobby lied and she hoped he wouldn't ask where because she hadn't made anything up yet. It wasn't really a lie though, she thought to herself, there were lots of other things she could be doing right now, especially things that would help her to uncover the truth about her grandmother.

"Oh, I see," he answered and Bobby was surprised to see that he looked quite crushed. This perplexed her even more. Why was he so determined to get to know her anyway? It was more than just wanting information from her, this she was sure of. She had never really known a boy before. She was an only child and all of her friends were girls. He certainly did seem a complex character. He looked away from her then and he had a distant kind of look on his face that she just couldn't understand.

He turned away from her and slowly began to walk off. Something about his way of walking made her feel so utterly sorry for him. She suddenly felt awful for being so rude to someone who was just trying to make a new friend, for whatever reason.

"Would you like to read some newspaper articles I found in my grandmother's attic that are over 50 years old?" she heard herself saying rather loudly. He turned to look at her and she noticed herself waving them about in the air and attracting the attention of the other people in the library. She stuffed them back into her pocket and walked to the 'quiet reading' section. David sat next to her on the couch and seemed very happy again.

Bobby was relieved for him but it did seem so strange to have a boy right next to her like this. She wondered what her mother and friends would make of it. Well, all of her friends were a long way away now in her old home town that they had just moved from. Bobby looked over to where the mothers were sitting. Daphne was there making quiet conversation with another mother. And then there was another woman, also with thick, curly black hair sitting by herself, knitting and presumably David's mother. There were also some smaller children sitting and playing with blocks and Leggo. They all seemed completely oblivious to the fact that Bobby and David were sitting together.

"I was just about to tell you," he said excitedly, "about a group of children that disappeared the same week of the alien craft sighting."

"Yes, I already know about that actually," Bobby said and pulled the newspaper article from her pocket. "I hope I'm not going to regret sharing this with you," she said and hesitated before she offered it to him.

"Scouts' honour and on my mother's grave," he made the scout's hand sign and then crossed his heart, "when she dies that is. Obviously she's not dead yet." He pointed to her. "I promise not to tell a living soul," he said earnestly. He took the newspaper and started to read.

"I don't believe it!" he said surprised. "Where on earth did you get these? They must be about 80 years old, and yes look, they are!" He was looking at the date. "And just look at this ... here's all of the missing children. There's old Henry Brewster and Ina Fairweather and well ... I don't recognise the others but they were all local children ... and it was all completely hushed up afterwards; that's the thing that baffles me. You know, this must be the only picture ever taken of those children. No-one ever talks about this. Apparently the whole town decided to just forget it ever happened so as not to upset the children any further. They all just wanted to get on with their lives, which you can understand I suppose ..." Bobby could see that David's mind was ticking over at a million miles an hour, as he read parts out and turned the articles over again and again.

"Yes, I know because Ina Fairweather is my grandmother. Her full name is Robina and her married name is Planks. She's my mum's mum and this has never been mentioned in our family."

"Right. So where did you say you got this," David suddenly remembered his earlier question, "if you don't mind me asking, that is?"

"No, not at all. We now live in the house that Ina lived in virtually all her adult life. I was looking through some of her things to try and find some clue to her life and I found this ... in the attic." She only just stopped herself from spilling out the rest of the details ... probably best not to talk of crystal balls and everything else just yet.

"Gosh and look at this!" Bobby was glad he had stopped her. "This is an article about my father's sudden appearance as a new-born baby on the doorstep of the Brewsters' house." He went quiet for a moment, his eyes popping from his head.

"My brothers and I have talked about this for years," he went on excitedly, "we know the Games adopted our father but we have always wanted to know where he came from. It's impossible for us to really know about our heritage because of this one missing link." He sat back on the couch with a thoughtful stare, ruffling the black curls on the top of his head quite roughly.

"If we could just find out how all of this is connected," he said, almost as if to himself. "There's got to be a connection between the tree, the missing children and the found baby ... but what?" He stared at her with his intense black eyes.

"Yes, I know," she said, looking away. "I have unanswered questions in my past too."

"Hmmmmm," he roused himself, "like what?"

"Well, my grandmother had a world of pain hidden behind that smile. She was happy enough on the outside anyway, but if you look carefully at her in the albums and photos scattered throughout her house you'll see there's always this sad look in her eyes. And she's often looking to the spot beside her as if there's someone missing. There's another strange thing too. She gave birth to my mother when she was 50. We're talking about the 1960s when people just didn't do that kind of thing. Can you imagine? Daphne's parents were in their early 60s when she was my age. Mum didn't like growing up with elderly parents and as an only child. She left as soon as she finished high school and rarely came back home until now, that is. And of course there's my father. Who on earth knows who that even was. It could have been an Italian waiter in Rome or a French artist in Paris or an English policeman in London ..." Now it was David's turn to be embarrassed. He swallowed loudly and said, "Hang on; go back a bit ... who's Daphne?"

"Oh, she's my mum," Bobby replied and he frowned at her. Then she realised what she had just said.

"Oh yes, I call her Daphne. I only call her Mum when we're around older people. It's too difficult for them to understand because they are a different generation to us."

Bobby stopped talking. She suddenly realised that she had probably given away too many family secrets and to someone she had only just met, too. She remembered what the Social Etiquette book that she had borrowed from the library had said: "One should always remember that we do not air our dirty laundry in public. A lady is expert at keeping confidences and speaking only of light and simple subjects." Thank goodness I don't have to worry about all of that in this day and age, she thought to herself. Still, family secrets should be kept within family and not for the first time she regretted that she had no idea of these things. Luckily for her David had a way of making her feel relaxed and she felt she could trust him.

"So okay ... how is it that you don't know who your father is?" He was blinking rather heavily and Bobby could see that he was having trouble grasping her very unconventional lifestyle.

"Oh well, that's because Daphne smoked a lot of pot and did all of those hippy things, you know, and well ...

she packed a lot of living into those 20 or so years after she left home and before she had me and so I guess she just doesn't really remember." Oh my God, Bobby thought to herself, I just did it again. I've just described my mother as if she was some kind of immoral floozy. She watched as David screwed up his face and then remembering himself he put on a phoney smile as if all of this was quite all right with him.

"Right," was all he seemed able to say as he scratched his head and rubbed his eyes in a nervous fashion. For the first time since meeting, Bobby noticed David was speechless.

"She's a really great person though. I'll have to introduce you to her one day," she added weakly, regretting how hideously honest she was with *everyone* and preparing herself for being judged on her mother's lifestyle, yet again.

They sat in silence. It was a long, uncomfortable silence. She could almost hear the cogs turning over in his head. Bobby was about to leave. She asked for the article back. She wouldn't sit with someone who would judge her mother without even really knowing her. Daphne was a wonderful person. Everyone who met her loved her instantly. She may have made some poor choices when she was younger but they seemed to only add to her great personality, not take away from it, or at least that was what Bobby thought anyway.

"You know, it's just occurred to me that we have had a similar thing happen in our families," David broke the silence almost in a whisper. "You see, my father was 67 when I was conceived which is quite old no matter what the year is. The thing is that he always looks so much younger than he actually is. Right now for example, he's still practising medicine full time and going about the place like an energetic 35 year old. People are always commenting on it and asking him for his secret ... it's almost as if that whole incident back in the 1930s somehow put these relatives of ours into some kind of time warp and ... well, who knows how it really happened? I would love to find out, wouldn't you?" Bobby agreed with him, saying, "Yes, I am very curious and would also love to know more."

"Well," he said at last, "aren't we a pair? Just think, the two of us meeting up like this, both of us having distant connections with this whole thing. What are the odds?" He smiled at her.

"I know," she answered, "but Daphne says there is no such thing as a coincidence. Everything happens for a reason. It's just a matter of figuring out what it is. I've also heard my mother say that people come into your life for a reason, a season or for life. And she uses big words like synchronicity and serendipity all the time. I *think* I know what she means ..." Now it was her turn to stare at him.

"Yes ... right, well, I hadn't really actually thought of it that way ... but it's an unusual way of looking at things and, um ..." David was stammering out his reply when right then they heard his mother call to him.

Then Bobby heard the librarian say to David's mother, in a shrill voice: "Please say hello to the doctor for me, Mrs Game."

"Shall do," answered David's mother and right at that moment Bobby realised that she had been talking to the local GP's son. They stood up for David to leave.

"May I?" he asked, holding his arms out towards her. For a moment Bobby thought he was going to hug her and she drew back. For some reason he had that offended look on his face again. She wasn't sure what he had meant, or what to do, so she offered him her hand for a good strong hand shake and said, "Yes you may," and then shook his hand vigorously. He looked disappointed.

"Would you like to see the tree with me?" he asked, still whispering. "We could meet there tomorrow, say at about 9am?"

"That should be all right," she said, mentally going through her schedule for the following day before realising that unravelling this mystery was now her most important priority. As she waved David goodbye, Bobby wondered at her total lack of feeling toward him when they had touched just now. She wasn't attracted to him in '*that* kind of way', which she was always hearing about but he did seem like a great person to know and she did have a special feeling that she couldn't work out just yet.

Her instincts told her though that in one way or another she would probably know him for a very long time, if not for life.

Chapter 4

THE MYSTERY OF THE OAK TREE

B obby walked for ten minutes from the town to the Brewsters' property and spotted David standing beside the enormous tree, waving to her. She resisted the urge to run to him, remembering that she was twelve now and that girls her age didn't do that kind of thing, so she took giant steps to get there quickly instead. He held out his arms as if to hug her again but she avoided that by running up to the tree and touching it. The trunk of the oak tree was absolutely massive. Much to her surprise there was a long, vertical opening in the tree that could house an adult or a couple of little kids at any rate. She'd never seen a tree quite like this one before and could now understand how people came to feel so enchanted by it. Indeed, just standing under it made you feel very relaxed, as if you were under some kind of magical spell.

David asked her to sit down with him on a picnic rug he had laid out on the ground. How very thoughtful, Bobby thought to herself and she noticed the flask of peppermint tea and plate of Anzac biscuits that he had made for her — such a delicious combination too. They spoke at length about everything they had learned recently and Bobby laid back to rest and soak up the beautiful spring day, basking in the shade of the magnificent oak and enjoying the company of her new friend. They stopped talking and Bobby felt David gazing at her. She noticed him smiling at her tenderly and that his movements had become dreamy and languid. She suddenly became very uncomfortable and sat up again. She smoothed out her skirt and continued talking.

"Right, so where were we?" she got back on track. "Yes, that's right; we're still hoping for some kind of clue to that mysterious thing that happened right here, this time 80 years ago," and she peered up into the endless branches. "Hmm, that's right. We're hoping for a miracle to come along and give us the answers we're looking for." He was still staring at her and smiling.

"Anyway," she said suddenly standing up, "there's no point just sitting around here is there? We're not really accomplishing anything. Thank you for showing me the tree and thank you so much for the lovely picnic but now I'd better be getting back home."

"Do you really have to go?" he asked, quickly packing all of the things into the hamper.

"I thought we'd spend some time together this morning, you know, trying to get some more information."

"What did you have in mind?" she asked, curiosity getting the better of her. As far as she could see they were at a dead end.

"Well, I did have an idea of what I wanted to do with you this morning but I wanted it to be a surprise. We need to head back into town though."

"Okay then," she answered frowning and wondering what on earth he could have planned. Once they were back in the town they went to the general store. Bobby noticed a figure slumped over by the side of the shop. He was wearing a long, worn-out and dirty coat and he looked very dirty. His head was hanging down so it almost touched his knees. She couldn't tell whether he was sleeping or not. Then she noticed that he was muttering away to himself, something about aliens.

She could tell by the state of him that he was a homeless person and her heart immediately went out to him. How could this be possible? Right here, only streets from where she lived in her own grand house, was someone who had absolutely nothing, not even a warm bed to sleep in. How could this be allowed to happen? How could the powers-that-be just turn a blind eye to this complete injustice? Why wasn't there some kind of service to provide for someone in this state? She made a vow to herself right then to go and volunteer at the soup kitchen this summer. She must have been wearing her emotions all over her face because David put his arm about her shoulder as if to steer her away from the old man.

"Yes, I know, the decay of our civilisation; it's awful isn't it?" he said, rather coldheartedly. Bobby looked at David, not able to believe he could be so casual about this. She was absolutely speechless. She told herself that later when she had a chance she would talk to David about what he had just said. In the meantime though David had gone ahead and ordered them each a chocolate milk shake. Why did he assume that she couldn't order and pay for her own drink or food? She took some coins out of her pocket and ordered a soya strawberry milkshake instead. This boy was really starting to annoy her. He stared at her, obviously not sure what he had done wrong.

"Well," she said angrily, feeling her temper prickling at her skin all over, "I don't drink cow's milk and I don't like chocolate and I'm able to order my own milkshake." She hoped that he didn't do or say anything else annoying now because she was just about to blow her stack at him.

"Sooorree," he answered sarcastically. Bobby pictured herself punching him on the nose at that moment but she took a deep breath and turned away from him to regain control. Her eyes settled on the man behind the counter who was making their drinks. He was looking at her as well but when their eyes locked he would look away. She noticed that he was an unusual looking fellow. He was quite short and extremely thin and was dressed in ragged green clothes. He wore a red cap on his head and his hair and beard were ginger and quite long. Bobby had seen him before somewhere and it bothered her that she couldn't quite remember where. The way he was looking at her, nodding his head and smiling, made her feel that he was just about to tell her something. But then he would look away and start humming to himself, a tune that Bobby had heard somewhere as well ... but from where? It was just on the edge of her memory. It all felt very strange.

"Why do you drink soya milk, Bobby?" David asked bringing her back to reality. He seemed to be sincerely interested in the answer and so she explained her reasoning.

"I don't like to drink the beverage that nature reserved for baby cows, that's all. I think it's inhumane to keep a cow pregnant and then take the calf from her so that humans can drink the milk, like she's some kind of machine. I prefer to drink milk made from the soya bean. It has all the same goodness." He frowned and started to blink heavily again. He thought about his answer very carefully. "Again, I had never quite thought of that in that way. You really think things through, don't you?"

She was puzzled by his response. Was that an insult? Judging by the friendly look on his face she would have to say no. At that moment the man brought their milkshakes around to the other side of the counter.

"So, what's this surprise?" she asked.

"Surprise? Oh yes, I'll take you soon; there's someone I want you to meet."

"Really? Is it anything to do with the tree and everything else we've been talking about?" Bobby couldn't help feeling as though he was going off the subject again.

"Kind of, I suppose," was his answer.

"I don't mean to be difficult David but we're supposed to be investigating the disappearance of eight children back in 1930s as well as the sighting of an alien space craft *and* the arrival of a baby from nowhere but instead we're here ordering milk shakes. I just don't get it and I guess I feel as if we're wasting time." Bobby wondered if David was taking this as seriously as she was. Right at that moment the man came around to the other side of the counter to give them the milkshakes.

"You know you shouldn't be going around talking about all of that," he whispered to the children, leaning over the bench and looking about to make sure no one else was listening. Bobby felt the presence of others at that moment and was quite sure she had seen many beings all around her and out of the corners of both of her eyes — but when she looked around, she realised that they were alone with the man in the store. She may have only seen them for a flash of a second but she was quite sure they were the same creatures she had seen in the attic in that dream. They both listened to what the man had to say. "I wouldn't go around talking about that subject unless you were hoping to stir up some trouble. Folks around here don't like people to talk about everything that happened back then."

"Yes, we've noticed that," David said.

Linda Maree Malcolm

"So where would we go if we wanted to get more information about all of that?" Bobby asked, ignoring the warning he had just given them. Something told her that this man could help her.

"Well, just between you and me and if anyone asks you, you didn't hear it from me, okay? That old man out there," he pointed to where the homeless man was sitting outside, "he has a firsthand, or now let me think, I suppose it's really a secondhand account of everything that happened on that night back in 1930 and it's all very interesting I might add."

David had no intention of making conversation with a homeless man. "Well thank you very much for your help," he said politely.

"Yes, thank you," said Bobby and without looking at David walked straight out of store to where the man was sitting.

"Excuse me," she said quite loudly, as he appeared to be in quite a deep slumber. "I'm sorry to disturb you but I heard you might be able to tell me more about the night of the alien ship sighting back in 1930."

"Wot's dat yer sayin'?" came the answer in a hiss.

"I said I'm sorry to have disturbed you but ..."

"Nah, nah, don' be sorry, now lass," he insisted, rousing himself "'ey, it looks like yor in da right place at da right time acause me ol' Da, God bless 'im, Samuel Rankin, jus' 'appened to be de ol' geezer 'o saw dat alien spacecraft. You can mark my words, missy; dat is no word of a lie. 'E was da one dat paper interviewed, like." He looked up at Bobby and she was able to see him properly at last. Even though he was toothless and smelt of a vile mixture of whiskey and filth she had a feeling she should listen to what he had to say. David appeared at her side and announced he was going home.

"Hang on, David," she said and pulled at his arm, "we'd love to hear the story, if that's okay," she said to the old man and hoped to herself that she wouldn't regret this.

* * *

"Or right den," said the old man but then he began to cough and splutter as if there was a fur ball stuck in his throat. "Aw, would ya look a' dat? Me 'ealth isn' wot it used to be, dats for sure."

"You don't say," said David sarcastically, but the old man seemed oblivious of him.

"Jus' when I goes ta tell me dory, me blasted t'roat goes an' closes right up on me, like. Ya jus' wouldn' read 'bout it would ya now?"

"Can I get you a drink? Would you like a milkshake?" Bobby offered kindly.

"I was tinkin' a bottle o' whiskey would be more me speed, lassie."

"Yes, of course it would be. Come on Bobby, we're wasting our time here," said David and he took Bobby's hand to lead her away. "It's okay," said Bobby to the old man, glaring at David to get him to hush up. This was their only chance to get a little more information.

"I'll get you some whiskey. Is there anything else?" she offered, much to David's total annoyance.

"Aw, would ya lass? Der's a good girl. An' ol' codger da likes a me gets a rumblin' in 'is tummy, ya know, bein' breakie time an' all. Dat would be grand, girlie. I'm tinkin' a roast beef roll with extra lashin's of gravy and can ya get me some more ciggies too luv? Marlboro is me fave."

"Certainly," said Bobby and the old man continued to do the fur ball cough.

"It's the least we can do," she whispered to David.

As Bobby was walking back into the store she saw what she thought were many streams of light twisted around one another, floating out through the doorway of the store and flying away into the sky. But she only saw it for a second and then it was gone leaving her blinking and telling herself it was just a sunray reflecting off something nearby. She heard the sound of laughter which gave her an odd feeling of deja vu.

When she entered the store she noticed immediately that it felt completely different to before and couldn't quite work out why. Then she noticed the man behind the counter. He was tall and heavily built, balding and wore a white apron.

"Hello, I was talking to the man who was behind the counter before about the ..." and she pointed toward the homeless man. His puzzled look made her stop and he shook his head.

"There's no-one here but me, missy. This is my store and I'm the only one here," he told her as he shuffled toward the back room. Bobby stood with her mouth open, unable to understand what she had just been told. She wanted to ask him more questions but realised it was pointless. Clearly he had no idea whom she was talking about.

In the meantime the old man outside tried to strike up a conversation with David. "My word, ya got yaself a fine one der, lad. An' she's a nice looker too and wif dat peachy ..."

"*Please ...*" David took a step away as if to leave.

"She's not my girl. She's my friend and I haven't 'got her' as you put ..." He couldn't tolerate the old man on any level and certainly would not put up with disgusting remarks regarding his newfound friend's lovely anatomy. He couldn't even think how to articulate to the man just how much he had offended him.

Bobby returned with what the old man had requested. The children then had to stand by and witness the man eating as if he hadn't eaten in weeks and then wash each mouthful down with the whiskey. As the man devoured the roll, gravy oozed into his moustache and beard and down his already filthy shirt front. David's sensibilities were severely offended beyond return and he had to turn and face the other way.

Every now and then the old man would look up at the children and mutter a food and whiskey-saturated "Yeah, an'" or an "I will tell ya, 'ang on". Bobby could see he was having great difficulty in eating the roll, chewing on his gums in his toothless mouth. He let out long exclamations of "Mmmmmmmmmm" periodically as well which also slowed down the whole process. At last the roll was devoured and he then proceeded to lick his fingers one at a time, thoroughly and over and over again until they were spotlessly clean.

David's face turned a light shade of green and he covered his mouth with his hand. Bobby giggled to herself. This was almost too much for poor old David to bear.

"Orrighty den," the old man finally said, "now where were I?" He opened his new cigarettes and lit one up. "Aw dat's right." He stood up then and taking a long inhale of the cigarette he blew the smoke full blast into David's face.

"That's disgusting," David said furiously, finding it was his turn to cough and splutter.

"Wot lad?" asked the old man

"You're enjoying this, aren't you?"

"What's dat lad?" the old man said and Bobby wondered if the old man had any sense at all of what others might think of him and his habits. Probably not, and he possibly wouldn't care anyway.

"Could we hear the story now?" she asked.

"Or right, but only for you, lass. Dat kid is far too serious fa me likin',"" and turning to David he said, "You're all uppity kid; wot's eatin' ya?"

"Please, just tell us your story. We have kept up our end of the bargain," Bobby pleaded.

"Yes, I must say, dat is true lass, I'll do it for you but not for 'im," he said pointing a backwards thumb to David.

"Now, where were I?" he said yet again. "Ah yeah, I 'members now, I do … me poor ol' Da; dis strange occu'rence 'appened to 'im, ya see, an' den 'e wos neva da same again."

The old man looked thoughtfully up to the sky as if he could actually see his father there.

"I'twern't acause 'e'd changed, aw anyting like dat. No i'twas dat all da peoples of dis town changed t'ward 'im afta da inc'dent. All a sud'en like, no one, not one single person took 'im seri'us anymore. I canna tink why e'ver. An it drove 'im mad as ya'd 'xpect. An' not one livin' soul in dis town, you mark my words now, b'lieved 'im an' then i'twas like dey kinda felt sorry for 'im or some'in.

But not e'nuff to give 'im a job or a chance like or ta 'elp 'im when da chips were down, which dey were of'en 'alieve me."

He stopped then and looked up to the sky again. He shook his head and wiped his eyes even though there were no tears there and then lit up another cigarette and blew smoke rings into the sky. He kept shaking his head as if in disbelief and then lit another cigarette from the one in his hand.

"Ahh, me poor ol' Da," he said finally, just when Bobby was beginning to think he would never get to the story. "I'm tearin' up, ya know, jus' tinkin' 'bout 'im. 'e was 'armless too, as 'armless as dey come ... anyway, I best be off den."

He took his cigarettes and stood up to leave.

"But," Bobby said in alarm, "you haven't told us the story yet."

"Wot 'tory's dat lass?" he asked earnestly.

"*The* story about what happened to your father on that night in 1930, remember?"

"Aw, didn' I tell ya dat part yet missy?" he sat scratching his head. "Ya have da forgive me lass, me mind's not as sharp as it used to be ... and," he took his hand to his throat, clasping it. "It's jus' dat me troat's closin' up agin, like. It needs summin' cold an' wet slidin' down it like."

"That's it! We're going. Can't you see there is no story? It's all a con job," David said, fuming and he took Bobby's arm and turned to leave.

"Oh orright, orright, sit down den an' I'll tell ya. Gawd, come on Mr Ser'us. Ya can't blame an' ol' codger like me fa tryin' it on now, can ya?" and he laughed long and hard and slapped his own knee, the tears rolling down his cheeks.

"Ya shoulda seen ya face jus' now lad. Ya look like I'm torturin' ya or sometin'."

Bobby didn't say anything at all but she could see by David's face that he did indeed feel tortured.

"So, okay den, where was I? Aw, yeah, dat's right. Me Da had a few too many bevies one night an' decided to walk it off up the Brewsters' lane. 'e couldna go 'ome, you know, not like dat or me Ma woulda chased 'im outta der wit' da broom." He stopped telling the story to have a little giggle to himself but then must have realised that the joke was lost on the children and so he continued on.

"Aw, da way me Da told it 'twas so funny. Anyways, 'e's walkin' down da road when off in the distance like, 'e see's all dese youngins' undoin' da gate at da Brewsters' property an' makin' dare way t'wards da mighty oak dat ev'ryone's always talkin' 'bout. 'Twasn't long after dat an' 'e saw from da spot where 'e was lyin' by da side of da road, like, d most pecul'ar ting." Bobby ignored David's visible flinching at the mispronunciation of most of the words.

"Low an' behold, all of a sudden like, de oak tree 'as dese 'uge lights dancin' all round an' spinnin', if ya can 'magine, kinda like a sideways ferris wheel. An' den all dese lightnin' strikes come flashin' out of da tree like, an' no thunder, min' you, jes' lightnin'. Dis went on for ages an' me Da couldna' work out if 'e was 'lucinatin', like, or what. Den 'e passed out from da shock of it like an' woke up da next day on da side o' da road an' took 'imself 'ome an' slept it orf. When 'e woke up later, me Ma told 'im 'bout da missin' chil'ren an 'e realised 'e 'adn't jes' been dreamin' an' dat i'twas de aliens orright dat came down an' took dose kids. 'e rang da paper and da cops straight away. 'e tort 'e was 'elpin'."

Linda Maree Malcolm

The old man went back to looking at the sky and shaking his head. They waited patiently, enthralled by the story and eager to learn more.

"Dat's right, lass, folks round 'ere don' like no one talkin' anytin' 'bout dis an' you know why don' ya? Acause dey are scared out o' dere wits dat dose al'ens will come back down 'ere and mess wiv 'em real bad next time. Dey are as frighten' as 'ell, you mark my words." He paused again. "An' dey won' like the likes of you two snoopin' 'round like, alieve me."

Bobby heard David click his tongue and wasn't sure if it was the threat of aliens that upset him or the use of the word 'like' three different ways in one sentence.

"An' I tell ya dis, too. Dos kids, aw dey came back orright but, as I sit 'ere livin' an' breavin', dos kids were neva da same aga'n. You could see it in dar eyes like, 'specially dat Ina girl." Bobby exchanged glances with David and they frowned at one another.

"Yes, go on," Bobby prodded.

"Well, 'twas as if dey had seen somein' really 'orrible like but either dey tweren' tellin' or they jes' couldna' remember. No one eva got to da bottom of it, eitha an' dat's how we jes know i'twas aliens, had da've been. Wot else could take da memory 'way like dat?" He started to cough again. It was clear to Bobby that the old man had come to the end of his story, but was probably about to ask for something else.

"Well, thank you so much for your time and your

incredible story, Mister. You have answered some questions for us but now I'd better be off. Goodbye," she said and shook his hand and she and David turned to walk home.

"Eh," he shouted out from behind her, "I tort you was diff'ent ta the likes of 'im. Not 'alf, mind, not 'alf!"

Bobby could hear him yelling all sorts of abuse. He must have planned to keep bribing them for things all day. She ignored him and was soon engrossed in conversation with David.

"Well, that was a complete waste of time," David told her.

"How can you say that? We have a story straight from the son of the only witness in this town of the whole thing. Don't you think that's something?"

"Yes, but how do we know it's even true. He is obviously a homeless drunk and who knows whether his word even counts for anything in this town anyway."

"I can't imagine why he would make something like that up; the whole story seemed very real to me. And besides, you make it sound like the way he has ended up is his own fault." Bobby was starting to feel irritated by David's obvious lack of compassion.

"Well of course it's his own fault," David retorted, looking more flustered than Bobby. "Every man is responsible for his own fate. You can't go on acting the victim and being a charity case forever. And besides, what does 'not 'arf' mean anyway? It's a stupid way of

Linda Maree Malcolm

talking. Only stupid people use the English language like that. It makes my ears feel like they are going to bleed."

"He had a good point though, didn't he David?"

"About what?"

"Why are you so uptight? I think it's a very good question."

She stopped walking and looked him straight in the eye. She couldn't stand his superior attitude any longer.

"What do you mean?" he demanded, "It's not that I'm uptight, as you put it, but that this is just logic, Bobby. If he got a job like everyone else and worked hard he could get himself out of this situation, couldn't he?"

"But maybe he can't get a job; maybe he has some mental problem or disease that holds him back. Maybe everyone is against him like he said. Don't you see how judgemental you're being? You don't know his story; in fact you don't know anything about him. Maybe he can't change for a very good reason and maybe he speaks like that because that was how he was raised to speak. You can't just go around putting everyone and everything into little boxes and labelling them."

"Gosh, Bobby, why are you taking his side anyway? For all we know it was *his* father who kidnapped those children. I mean, we just don't know, do we?"

"Oh my God, you are impossible!" Bobby turned to walk away from him. She could feel her temper building and she knew from past experience that it wasn't going to be pretty if she lost it. She would say something she regretted later, for sure. Count to ten, she told herself, count to ten and hold your temper, Bobby.

"Is it because you've got Celtic roots too, is that it Bobby? Come back so we can talk!" he shouted, equally furious. She didn't turn back. What she wanted to say was that she thought he was a snob who took his privileged upbringing for granted but she didn't want to have to be the one to say that. It was better for him to work that out for himself. She took giant steps all the way home and when she closed the front door behind her she breathed a sigh of relief and was glad to be in her quiet home alone once more.

Chapter 5
DECISION TO ACT

Bobby was in two minds about seeing David again. She couldn't imagine how she could be friends with someone who was so different to her. But her reservations were soon forgotten when he arrived on her doorstep the next day, apologising sincerely for the way he had acted.

"Can't we just try to put aside our differences at least until we have a solution to our puzzle? I see how you were right about how I do have neat little categories for everything. It is true, I admit that. But Bobby, what you have to understand is that this is the way I've been brought up. My father and grandfather were doctors and all of my seven older brothers were educated at universities and went on to become doctors, lawyers, newspaper journalists and so on. They are all self-made men. Even my mother, who is the only female in my life, is bookish and a published author of science reference manuals. We sit at the dinner table for hours and talk about world news, the stock market and politics.

"So ..." Bobby couldn't imagine where this was going.

"We have done that ever since I can remember; it's the world I grew up in and it's who I am," explained David, desperate for her to have a better understanding of his life.

"So what's that got to do with you? Does your whole family hate anyone who doesn't measure up to their own standards and if so do you have to be a sheep?" she demanded. She could see that he was confused now. He blinked heavily and frowned at her. "It's not that they hate people but they have a very strong work ethic that's all. There's nothing wrong with that and I don't want to be different to that ... I think."

"Okay, I do understand David, I really do. But surely you see that it's only that you have the parents and grandparents that you have, that you have those privileges." He looked at her puzzled.

"You can't blame someone for something that he had no control over; do you see what I mean?" Bobby persisted, "Just because they are born into a different family than yours, is that their fault? In fact we can even go as far as saying that it was just sheer luck that you were born into the family that you were born into, but that doesn't make you better or smarter than anyone else." She waited for him to absorb this information.

"Yes, well to be honest there have been times in my life where I have had some moments of insight but I suppose in the end I am very limited because of the way my parents have brought me up." He sat and stared at the floor and paused for a moment as though deep in thought. "But now you've got me thinking about new things, Bobby, which is good. I mean, just think if I had never met you I might have gone the rest of my life not realising what a complete and utter snob I am *and* that it really isn't right for cows to have to give the milk for their calves to humans *and* that we all have a unique destiny and are not necessarily here to just float about on the breeze." She could see that he was becoming excited with all of this new information. "So can I assume you realise what a hypocrite you've been as well?" she teased.

"How's that?" he asked earnestly.

"You say it's not right for a man to blame his background or upbringing for his circumstances and yet that is exactly what you just did." He smacked his hand to his mouth in horror and then started to laugh. They both laughed then and the tension between them dissolved. Then he knelt down in front of her and spoke in Italian, appealing for her forgiveness.

"Mi dispiace, perdonami, spero che si puo essere amici."

"You don't have to beg me," she said even though she had no idea what he had just said. His eyes said it all. She could feel the colour rising into her face and yet somehow she could also feel herself softening towards him. He took her hand in his and, looking into her eyes, said, "I'm not begging, but will you forgive me and still be my friend?"

"Yes, of course. I'm sure I make mistakes too and I'm constantly learning new things from you as well, so I guess it's a two-way street, isn't it?" she said quickly and then snatched her hand back. Italians seemed to have no idea of personal space.

"What's wrong?" he asked.

"I think you should have some background information about me too. You see I have spent a lot of years travelling all over the world with Daphne to some very exotic places and my childhood has been far from normal. I've learnt about all kinds of different cultures and religions and have taken little pieces from each to become the person that I am today. My mother's main area of interest is spirituality and all that it involves." She stopped to light a stick of incense and put it on the table beside her. "I can talk about chakras, mediumship, meditation, yoga and clairvoyance all day long because that's what I've been taught about. That's what I know." She paused to catch her breath. She could tell from the look on his face that he had no idea what she was talking about.

"I'm sorry to have to say this, Bobby, but I've been brought up to believe that unless something can be proven scientifically then it just doesn't exist, unless we're talking about something that's in the minds of lunatics and Satanists. But now I can see that it's time to open my mind more and Bobby ..." he looked at her imploringly, "I'd like to be a student in your world but maybe there are things that I can teach you too."

"Yeah, sure," she said smiling. She was relieved to be talking all this through.

"We have an agreement then. Shake on it." He offered his hand and they shook hands.

"So where's your mum right now?" he asked.

"She's with a client in the kitchen."

"A client?" he asked.

"Yes, she's doing an angel card reading." She noticed his apprehension.

"Oh don't worry; she won't come riding in here on a broomstick and take your eyeballs for her latest spell."

David was taken aback at first but then he realised she was joking and he relaxed again.

"Okay ... so what is an angel card reading?" She could see he was really trying to learn.

"Right, well it's where Daphne lays out her cards for a client and then, by looking at the pictures and tuning into the voice of her guides, can tell them exactly what is coming up for them in their future."

"Right and what are 'guides' then, may I ask?"

"Yes of course. Guides are spiritual beings that live in the ether and communicate with each and every one of us all of the time. If you develop your psychic muscle, which we all have by the way, you can tune into the voice of your guide and you can learn about all kinds of things." Bobby hoped that this explanation wasn't too weird for him.

"Right ... I see," he said frowning and clearly he didn't

see at all. He began to scratch his head and rub his eyes again.

"Look I'll show you," Bobby said and picked up her cards from the table beside her. She would give him a demonstration.

"So, you're telling me that you can tell my future right now just by looking at some cards? Are the guides talking to you right now?" he asked incredulously.

"Yes, I have the gift too. If I just take a moment to centre myself," she said, taking a deep breath and then she held the cards to her chest and laid them out.

"Yes, I see. It says here that you are going to be sent away to boarding school soon because eventually you're hoping to be a scientist of some sort, maybe a marine biologist or something like that and of course there are no schools around here. It also talks of the fact that your mother homeschools you because she wishes to protect you from the local children who she fears may have a negative impact on you." Bobby also saw other things too, such as the fact that he had just met a girl with whom he felt a strong connection. She chose not to mention that though. It would be too awkward as she was quite sure that the girl was her. It was times like this that Bobby almost regretted her gift. To see such deep emotion laid out in the cards ...

"What? How can that be?" He glanced around the room and then picked up each card to look underneath it and on its back.

"It's all right here," Bobby said, smiling.

"Yes, but you've just worked that out by sorting through all of the other information I've already given you about me — and the rest was just a lucky guess," he insisted, at the same time checking underneath all of the cards all over again.

"Ha, I knew it was impossible for you to change. I was right," she pounced.

"No, no, no, not at all. Okay yes ... I suppose you're right. But I am trying to understand Bobby; you've got to give me that."

"Yes, at least you're trying. That's good. But now I want to try you with something else." She hadn't intended on showing anyone the crystal ball as yet but before she knew it, she had become swept up in the moment.

"I'll be back in a minute," she said as she bounded up the stairs. She really had longed to have someone with whom to share her discovery, she had to admit to herself. When she sat down again, she was quite breathless.

"Where did you go?" he asked curiously. She took the ball out from inside her jacket and held it up in front of their faces so they could have the best view of it.

"What!" David exclaimed, "It's beautiful. What is it? Where did it come from?"

"Well, you'll never guess," answered Bobby excitedly. "I found it with the newspaper articles in the attic of this house."

"It's extraordinary. What is it?"

"Yes it is and I've just been dying to tell someone. It's a crystal ball, used to tell the future. I have a feeling my grandmother, Ina, had the gift as well although why this has been hidden away in the attic, I can't say."

"Yes. And look at this beautiful fancy writing. What does it say?" David leant in close to the ball to decipher the old fashioned print.

"Oracle in the Mist," he said, quite loudly and clearly. "What on earth does that mean?"

Right at that moment the mists started to swirl within the crystal ball as they had done the day before when Bobby had found it.

"What's happening?" David asked, jumping back in the seat and sounding alarmed.

"I wish I knew," answered Bobby, equally alarmed. "This happened when I was looking at the ball the other day too but I convinced myself that I was just imagining it."

"How peculiar," David said as he took the ball and turned it upside down and all around. Again the mists exited the ball and began to swirl all around the room.

Suddenly the children heard the ball calling their names, quietly at first and then louder and with more intensity, *"Bobby-David-Bobby-David-Bobby-David!"*

"This can't be happening," David said. "You're playing some kind of trick on me, aren't you Bobby? Tell me that's what this is?" But he could see by the shocked look on her face and the way that she was recoiling back on the couch as well that she was just as surprised and scared as he was.

"Bobby-David-Bobby-David-Bobby-David!" it went on and on.

"How can it possibly know our names? This can't be …" David muttered as he was determined not to believe what was happening, but then the ball said, *"Bobby, David, go to the oak tree tonight at 9 o'clock!"* over and over until David said, "Quickly, just put it away and see if it stops then!"

They put some cushions on it which stopped the voice immediately. The mists disappeared. They sat frozen to the spot, staring at one another in amazement. Bobby was the first to break the silence.

"What just happened?" she whispered, as if not wanting the ball to hear.

"I have no idea. This is the strangest thing to have ever happened to me. How on earth did it know our names … I just don't get it?"

"Yes and what was all of that about the oak tree?"

"I have no idea, but one thing's for sure, there's no way I'm ever looking at that ball or going to the oak tree again. God only knows what dangers we could be getting ourselves into," David said adamantly.

"Well," Bobby said after taking a moment to think, "I understand you're afraid, David, but just think, here we are trying to uncover the mystery surrounding our family members and we now have an opportunity to do just that. Going to the tree tonight might just bring us one step closer to our goal."

"That's crazy, Bobby," David said. "Do you realise what we could be getting ourselves into?"

"Yes, I think I do and do you know what? Even if you don't go I'm going to. I'm not afraid," Bobby said defiantly. She was never one to back down from a challenge.

David could see by the look on her face that she was deadly serious. He knew her well enough by now to know that there was no point arguing with her and no way of talking her out of it. He shook his head.

"You're crazy!"

"Maybe I am," she smiled at him. She was going and that was all there was to it.

David wondered what she was getting him into this time. He had no choice but to follow along with her. He would feel awful if something were to happen to her and he wasn't there to help her out. After all, that's what friends were for, right?

Chapter 6
BOBBY TAKES THE PLUNGE

That night, Bobby told her mother that she was going out for ice cream with her new homeschooler buddy. It was daylight savings and spring and so it wouldn't be getting dark for some time yet. David didn't have to think of an excuse at his home because everyone was out at various meetings, dinners or on business trips.

Bobby and David met at the general store and started the walk to the Brewsters' property. They were equally apprehensive and excited and talked rapidly about what they expected to happen at the oak tree.

"That reminds me," Bobby said, "what was the surprise you had for me yesterday?"

"It was nothing really," David said. "It wasn't anything to do with all of this." He made a gesture with his hands which must have referred to their investigation around the tree. "My parents were both at home yesterday and I was hoping to introduce you to them. Mum had actually asked you for lunch as well. We were having lasagne with home-made pasta sheets."

Bobby felt awful now about their difference of opinion

Oracle in the Mist   57 the day before and was glad that they had managed to get it sorted out. She could see how disappointed David was too.

"I really am sorry about that David," Bobby said sincerely. "I think it sounds like a lovely idea to meet your parents and the thought of home-made lasagne is making my mouth water just thinking about it." She touched his hand for a moment to let him know that she cared and that she meant what she said, which seemed to cheer him up instantly. Was it that he did have deep feelings for her or was this how all Italians were towards their friends, she thought to herself. She really had no idea, having never met an Italian before. They smiled at one another.

"Did you bring the ball?" David asked.

"Yes, I thought I should as it might be about to give us more instructions. I also brought water, crackers, cheese, bread and apples."

"Excellent and well thought out. Good girl."

Bobby cringed to herself. On the one hand she liked the fact that she had pleased her new friend but there was something creepy about being told "good girl". She felt annoyed and she couldn't quite figure out why. They arrived at the tree in silence.

"Well, here we are again," he said from underneath the tree, staring up into the mighty and many branches. "What do we do now?" she asked, looking at her watch. It was 8.55pm and the Oracle had said to arrive at 9 o'clock.

"I have no idea," he answered. "Get the ball out and put it underneath the tree there and we'll see what happens."

They took it out of the black velvet bag that Bobby had found for it and placed it on the ground and then stood staring at it for quite some time. 9 o'clock came and went and still nothing happened.

"This isn't right," David said at last. "We must be missing something because the mists aren't swirling like they were this afternoon. It's as if we have to activate it somehow. Just think, what was it that we did this afternoon that we haven't done now?"

"Yes, this is strange. There are no mists and there's no Oracle talking," agreed Bobby.

Right at that moment, the mists started to swirl and Bobby and David looked at one another and said simultaneously, "Aaah!"

"I see," said David, "you have to say the words on the ball to activate it."

Then they heard the familiar voice, *"Bobby, David, Bobby, David,"* and then, *"Are you there; are you there?"*

Bobby and David looked at one another in bewilderment and then the voice spoke again, *"Bobby, David, step into the tree! You have to step into the tree together."*

"What?" said David, nervously, "Step into *that* tree? I don't think so." He began to back away. But Bobby picked up her backpack and the crystal ball and walked around to the other side of the tree.

"What are you doing?" he yelled at her. "You can't be serious? You have no idea what's going to happen. It's too dangerous Bobby."

"I know David, but do we really have a choice? I mean really, we have this opportunity; we can't just walk away from it. Come on David, what could possibly go wrong?" She used her free hand to feel around inside the hole of the tree. No spiders or other creepy insects — that was a good sign.

"Come on Bobby; don't do this. If something were to happen to you I'd never forgive myself. I'm responsible for you, you know?"

"Oh, pooh, pooh, David Game," she snapped back. "I'm responsible for myself and anyway how did you ever get the notion that you're responsible for me? I mean, really ..." Bobby frowned at him.

"It's not meant to be a rude thing. Please don't argue with me, Bobby but you are the fairer sex and it's the boy's job to protect because we are just stronger ..."

"God, David! Are you stuck in the dark ages? Haven't you ever heard of a girl being bright enough and strong enough to protect herself? Goodbye David Game ..." Bobby said — and with that she stepped into the tree and vanished.

"What?" David stared in disbelief. "This can't be happening. Where did she go?" Right then he heard an ear-splitting sound and looked up. There were lights darting everywhere, above the tree, as if giant fireflies were having a dance off and then the lightning began again. It came from the clouds above and bounced off the uppermost branches of the tree.

"What ... what ... Bobby, stop fooling around!" David said as he ran around the tree several times but there was no sign of her. This must have been some kind of magical, witchcraft stunt that she had pulled and she would turn up again in a minute, right? But the minutes ticked by and then the thought occurred to him that this was for real. She wasn't coming back.

"Bobby," he yelled again, "what are you getting me into this time?" He looked into the hole in the tree and could feel a sob coming up from his chest, threatening to overwhelm him.

"No good crying David," he said to himself out loud. "There's only one thing for it then I suppose. This is just typical Bobby style, isn't it? She says she doesn't need rescuing and yet here I am, the only one who can rescue her. God, I hope I don't regret this."

And with that he ran into the tree at full pace. If he had been there to see it, David would have noticed that the lightning strikes and flashing lights above the tree looked just like an alien space craft.

Chapter 7
PROFESSOR LAMBERT AND SEBASTIAN

Meanwhile, Bobby woke up to find herself in very strange surroundings. She had no idea what had just happened. The last thing she remembered was stepping into the tree but she did remember bright lights and lightning flashes ...

She had to fight off a sob of panic. What had she gotten herself into? She already regretted that she had mocked David and would do anything to be with him again. She would cling to him and never let him go. What if she never saw him again? What if she never got home again?

"David, are you here too?" she whispered, hoping for a response. She glanced around the room. She could see that she was in a hut of some sort made from bamboo and palm fronds. The floor was sandy and there was no furniture to speak of. Right then she became aware of the fact that she was fully clothed and lying in a bed. She felt behind herself, just to be sure. She felt sweet relief when she touched the coarse canvas of the backpack. At least she would have something to eat if she was all alone.

Then her hand was drawn to something warm in the bed beside her. She quickly pulled her hand back when she realised that it was a living, breathing form lying beside her.

She closed her eyes and felt herself freeze in terror; the seconds ticked by like hours. She couldn't bring herself to look behind her. That could be anything lying right next to her. Then she heard the quietest whisper.

"Is that you, Bobby?" She recognised David's voice and was quite certain there had never been another time in her life that she had felt so glad.

"Yes," she said and turned around, slipping off the backpack.

"Where on earth are we?" he said still whispering.

"I've got no idea David, but I'm telling you, I'm so glad to see you." She threw her arms around him and kissed him on his cheek.

"What have you got us into this time Bobby Fairweather?" he asked and hugged her to him as well. "Have you got any idea what we just did?" he asked Bobby, looking both scared and excited. Bobby remembered then that David was a science fiction nut and was constantly talking about journeys to the centre of the earth and time machines and she assumed he had an extensive library at home which featured all of his favourite books. Now she found herself feeling grateful for this interest because he might have an explanation for what had just happened.

Linda Maree Malcolm

"No, no idea," she answered.

David continued, "It looks to me as if we just travelled through a wormhole to another dimension or even," and he paused and looked around again, wide-eyed, "even a parallel dimension."

"I'm so glad you followed me in David. I wouldn't want to be here by myself," Bobby confessed, surprising even herself at with the words that were coming out of her mouth. She gave him a little hug.

"But I thought you didn't need protecting ..." David teased.

"Oh, I don't need rescuing or protecting — but just for company, you know ..."

"Oh sure, I know," he went along with her. He looked down at her and they both burst out laughing.

"Hey, at least we've got some cheese. If nothing else, we won't go hungry"

"That's great," he agreed, "and in the meantime, let's try to figure out how *we* did the very thing that scientists have been trying to do for hundreds of years."

"I'd love to help you figure that out David, but right after we have something to eat I need to work out how to get back home. My mum's going to be worrying about me." Bobby suddenly became aware of the reality of the situation. "And besides, we could be killed at any given minute. I say we get out of here."

"Hey, this was your idea, Bobby. I just followed you. It's a bit late to be regretful. Anyway, I don't think we were lured here by that voice to be eaten or killed. No. Whoever it was that was calling us, knows us, somehow. I have a feeling this is where the children came when they disappeared back in 1930."

Bobby saw the sense in what David was saying and relaxed a little. David stood up.

"Let's look around a little," he said and went to a small window and looked out. It was broad daylight with a clear blue sky and the sun was shining. In the distance was an ocean.

They both suddenly became aware of huge waves being smashed upon a shoreline and then they heard something else — voices talking to one another and coming towards the hut. Bobby cringed inside with fear but her ears pricked up as well.

"Well, I can't see any point in doing that; they'll be here sometime soon; I am sure."

"Orr, orr, orr, screech, screech," came a most peculiar noise. The two voices seemed to be communicating with each other.

"What! Oh Sebastian, that's preposterous! No they're not going to end up in another time zone so don't even think about that. This is the *only* time zone. Remember, that's what the Oracle said. No we'll stay with our original plan and ... quiet now, we'll take a look inside and see if they've arrived."

David took Bobby's hand and stood slightly in front of her as if to shield her.

"Screech," came the response in the strange language.

"Indeed, Sebastian," whispered the male voice and then the hut door opened and in stepped a tall, lean, middle-aged man and a monkey.

"Orr, orr, orr, orr, screech," said the monkey.

"Quite right, Sebastian, quite right. I told you, the Oracle is never wrong. Professor Lambert, at your service," he said, to the children, bowing slightly in the same way that David would.

"Orr, orr, orr," said the monkey, looking up at the professor.

"Oh, terribly sorry old chap; getting a bit carried away, aren't I? This is Sebastian, most esteemed colleague, assistant and scholar in his own right. We are most pleased to be finally meeting you and to be making your acquaintance," and they both bowed again. Bobby and David stood motionless and speechless.

"I take it your names are Bobby and David," said the professor, sensing their apprehension. "Oh yes, we've been expecting you for some time now ... some time ... let me see, I think it equates to 80 years your time ..." he said and looked thoughtful.

"But how ... and why ..." David attempted to put all of his jumbled thoughts into one question.

"Well, it's quite simple really. Ah, so many questions and so much time. I expect you want a lengthy explanation to all of this?" the professor said and gestured with his hand by waving a 180 degree circle of the hut. "Now I don't know about you, old chap," he said and stepped forward and shook David's hand very fast and then clapped him on the shoulder in a friendly way, "but I personally think that an occasion such as this calls for some tea, don't you?" He then gestured towards the door.

The children looked at one another as they were being ushered out of the door. Outside, the bright sun blinded them for a moment and they each stood blinking. When Bobby was able to finally open her eyes properly she found herself rubbing them over and over again just in case what she thought she saw was not what was actually before her. It was in utter amazement that she realised that it was all very real and not some kind of a dream after all.

What she was looking at was more incredible than any scene she had ever seen in any movie. It almost defied description. Dark-skinned people and all kinds of animals were walking about, sitting with one another and doing all kinds of crafts together. They were selling to one another in a market place and still others were sitting and picnicking with each other. Children were mingled in amongst the animals and adults and played games with each other like hopscotch and knuckles.

It took a moment to take it all in and then Bobby realised what it was that was so alarming about what she was seeing, as a large, poisonous looking snake slithered through the crowd and on into the bush. Lions sat and were patted by babies and tigers and leopards walked

Linda Maree Malcolm

around without a care in the world and certainly not looking as though they were about to make a meal of any of the people. There was harmony and serenity between the people and the animals. It was quite extraordinary.

"Ina, Ina and Henry! Ina and Henry!" People started to point at the children and shout out the familiar names.

And then they were rushed at by a large group of natives who clamoured around them, and reached out to touch them or just stood staring at them, smiling warmly. Other natives insisted on kissing them and wrapping their arms around their shoulders in the warmest and most tender way. It didn't feel threatening at all, thought Bobby. In fact it was quite pleasant.

"Hello. You are back, yes, yes?" was the question that was being constantly asked of them. All thoughts of getting home to Daphne or worries about where and how they had ended up in such a place left the mind of Bobby. She suddenly became aware of the professor trying to convince the people that their names were Bobby and David, not Ina and Henry.

"Yes, I know it's remarkable, I agree. The resemblance is just remarkable; quite a shock in fact," and even the professor stood back to marvel at them, smiling and clicking his tongue in awe. Then Bobby heard a question being spoken that seemed to reverberate throughout the gathering and suddenly everyone became quiet as they awaited the answer.

"The baby? Where's the baby?" one of the natives

asked and Bobby and David looked to the professor simultaneously for an explanation.

"I assure you that there is an answer to every one of your questions," the professor said politely, "but first be so kind as to allow me to spend some time with these lovely young people who have just arrived and in time all will be revealed. Do we have an agreement ... please?" He then gestured that Bobby and David should be allowed to pass through the crowd and the people parted to allow them through. Bobby and David moved through the crowd and started to ascend a narrow, sandy path that disappeared into the jungle.

"Right, now where were we?" the professor asked. "Ah yes, we're setting off to my place for that cup of tea. Splendid idea, even if I do say so myself."

Bobby and David each had thoughts racing through their minds as they made their way to the professor's house. Going off into the jungle with a virtual stranger went against everything they had both ever been taught but in their hearts they knew that they were safe and that there was nothing to worry about.

The path passed through a fern glade that was so lush as to be dripping and then they found themselves walking on the softest and greenest moss they had ever seen. They next started to climb tiny steps that zigzagged up and up until finally they reached the plateau where they found themselves standing under a massive house supported underneath by gigantic bamboo stilts.

Linda Maree Malcolm

The professor pointed behind them and each of the children turned at the same moment to look and see a view that was so incredible that they each inhaled sharply — an immense sparkling aqua ocean spread out as far as the eye could see. The blazing sun shining on the water made it seem as if diamonds were jumping from the water in all directions. But it wasn't just the water that was completely mesmerising. It was what was going on *above* and *in* the ocean that was most astonishing. Sea creatures floated through the water and jumped from it. Bobby could have sworn she was looking at the Loch Ness monster and whales and dolphins leaped from the ocean effortlessly. And above the ocean, the sky was just as busy. Birds of all shapes and sizes flew all about.

David recognised that many of them were not species found in their own world and were probably what they would call "prehistoric". Bobby and David looked at one another and then at the professor incredulously.

"This is beyond anything ... How can this be ..." asked David, struggling to find the right words.

"Yes, all in good time, my lad. Now let's make haste."

They all turned to continue walking up another flight of tiny steps when the most peculiar thing happened. Coming down the steps, towards them, was a procession of cats of all shapes, sizes and colours. Not just any old cats — no, there were all kinds of cats! There were lions, tigers, leopards, and domestic cats too. Tabby cats and hairless cats. And even sabre tooth cats and other cats that the children had no name for in their own language. All magnificent creatures and all coming towards them. Bobby became frightened but the professor reassured her that there was nothing to be alarmed about. The cats would make their way straight past them.

"Oh yes, how silly of me. Dratted memory," the professor said, smacking his own head. "I'd completely forgotten about the cat meeting being held up there at the meeting place this morning. Well, I certainly do hope they have reached a workable solution to their problem."

Bobby could see that David was about to ask "What problem?" when the foremost lion, who had reached the bottom step and was right next to them, let out an almighty roar. David held Bobby's hand again and stood in front of her. She found herself starting to like this idea of the boy protecting the girl, but then told herself to stop being so silly.

"Extraordinary!" exclaimed the professor as if to answer the lion.

"So very pleased for you and such incredible progress; good for you," he said, again to the lion and he gave the lion a low bow and then, with his hand, gestured for the lion and his company to proceed down the stairs.

"After you, kind sir," he said to the lion. The lion stood up from resting on his rear legs and after letting out one more earth-shattering roar, set off down the stairs with his following behind him.

"Orr, orr, orr, screech," said the monkey to the professor.

"Yes, I know. I really am terribly pleased for them, old chap, aren't you? An excellent outcome and I really must say that I'm rather staggered that they've finally found a solution. Completely unprecedented. What a most wonderful day this is shaping up to be — and not just any old day either, but a very special day in the history of our island!"

"Screech," said the monkey.

"Quite right, Sebastian, quite right," agreed the professor.

Bobby had to resist the urge to start laughing hysterically at this point. It wasn't just the fact that the professor seemed to be able to communicate with animals or that there were prehistoric creatures roaming around or even that there was complete harmony between the animals and the people or the fact that she had apparently just time travelled to another dimension with a boy she hardly knew, leaving behind her mother who would probably be frantic with worry about her daughter by now. No, it wasn't any of that.

The thing that amused her the most and made her cover her mouth with her hand to stop the giggle from erupting and making her appear rather rude was the attitude of the cats. Apparently cats are the same in all time dimensions. Each and every one of the cats marched past the small gathering with an air of superiority, tails and noses up in the air, eyeing the children nonchalantly as if they had not the slightest bit of interest as to who they were or where they had come from. They obviously had far more important things to tend to. In fact there may have even been a slight air of distaste from the cats towards the small group. The last tiny furless cat, who was quite ugly by anyone's standards, gave an aristocratic flick of its head as if to dismiss them completely and proceeded to make its way down the stairs. Such an air of royalty, Bobby had never seen before, not even displayed by the royalty of her own world. The professor continued to bow low to the cats as they passed and as soon as the last one was away down the mountain the little group made their way to the entrance of the professor's house.

Chapter 8
MYSTERY OF THE EIGHT REVEALED

On entering the professor's house, the children were stunned by how much was packed into the four walls. While the hut they had awoken in was completely empty this one was the exact opposite. It seemed as if not one more thing could be jammed into this house. Both Bobby and David expressed their surprise at the sheer volume of books lining shelves all around the inside of the house and also acting as free-standing room dividers. Bobby thought that there were probably more books here that she had ever seen in any library. It would take weeks or even months of snooping and investigating to see everything that this house held. There were a lot of areas that were cluttered with old rubbish and had been left so the dust had built up but even that did not diminish their enthusiasm. Many nooks and crannies were appealing to the children and they both had to fight the urge to run off and start exploring the house.

"Oh, be my guests," said the professor, as if he could read their minds. The children looked at each other gleefully and took off in separate directions. Bobby found herself drawn to a sketch of a woman that hung on a wall by the window.

For a moment Bobby thought she recognised the woman, but no, it was probably just her imagination playing tricks on her again, but still she couldn't help staring at it. There was definitely something about the eyes ...

"Ah, yes, I thought you might notice that. Beautiful, isn't she? How is Daphne anyway?" but as soon as the words were out of his mouth, he clapped his hand to his mouth and said in a whisper repeatedly, "Shut up old fool, oh shut up, what have you done, silly old fool, taboo subject, remember?"

"What was that?" Bobby asked, becoming intrigued. Could it really be her mother?

"What?" he said calmly and turned away as though to ignore her.

"You just mentioned my mother's name, Daphne."

"What's that? Your mother's name? No I didn't. No, I said, 'Lousy artist, what a shame!'" the professor insisted.

"But I heard you ... just now," Bobby persisted.

"Your mother ... why would I ask about her? I have no idea who she is." Even though Bobby had just met the professor, she could tell by the way he avoided looking at her and stood gazing out of the window with his hand on his hip, humming a tune nervously to himself that he was lying.

76   Linda Maree Malcolm

"Screech," said the monkey.

"Oh good heavens, yes Sebastian, I'd quite forgotten. Time to make the tea. Excuse me," the professor said and he bowed slightly and turned to take the whistling kettle off the boil. Bobby and David stared at one another, puzzled. David had heard the reference to Daphne too. David shrugged his shoulders to show Bobby that he found it quite mysterious as well.

"Right. Time for tea. Aahh, are there any better words in the English language?" the professor said becoming quite excited at the prospect of having a fresh pot of tea. He stirred the pot enthusiastically and then poured the amber liquid straight into cups already prepared with milk and sugar. He handed it to the children. It was quite delicious. Very creamy and sweet. He also offered them some Anzac biscuits.

"So, have you met my mother then?" Bobby took up her line of questioning from before.

"You know, I've just this moment realised that these blasted tassels that have been the bane of my life for, oh, let me think ... too many years to remember, can easily be detached." He took the moccasin from his foot and held it up to demonstrate. "You see, every time I move my feet about, when I'm walking for instance, they bounce and bob around in the most annoying fashion." He was staring at the slipper intensely.

"Screech," said Sebastian.

"My sentiments exactly, old chap. I believe I have

stumbled onto the solution. See how tea gets the old grey matter working. Remarkable! Now all I have to do is snip them off," and again he demonstrated by pretending his fingers were the scissors and snipping at the base of the tassels. "Now where did I put those scissors? Let me think. Oh, that's right!" He smacked the side of his own head. "I lent them to those dratted natives decades ago and it's my guess that they never returned them." He let out a long sigh. "Fantastic people but simply no idea how to care for *things* and so unreliable in that way, you know, with things that you or I just take for granted. I'll bet those scissors are lying buried somewhere all rusted up and underground by now. Still …"

David and Bobby looked at one another blinking heavily. Something told them they had just stumbled into the drawing room of the most eccentric professor that ever lived. David went to ask a question but the professor overruled him by talking loudly over the top of him.

"I could use my pocket knife. Splendid idea, old chap." He seemed to be talking to himself now. "Now where is it, I wonder? Oh that's right." He jumped up from his spot, one slipper in hand and the other on his foot, and sweeping up the knife, opened it and severed off the tassels all within a few seconds.

"There," he said, most pleased with himself and the look of the new moccasins. "So incredibly easy and quite liberating, if I do say so myself. I can't think why I didn't do it years ago." He walked around in the slippers in circles, grinning from ear to ear.

"Right, now ... where were we?" he asked the children and took his seat again, smiling hugely and marvelling at his moccasins.

Bobby and David exchanged glances again and David frowned and shook his head at Bobby as if to imply she should discontinue her line of questioning.

Whatever the truth was about Daphne, it would have to wait. Obviously for some unknown reason, the professor was not comfortable discussing it. Bobby sat on her hands and chewed her bottom lip furiously. She felt as though she was being ignored and she didn't like that feeling, not one little bit. She held herself back from shouting the thing that was on the tip of her tongue which went something like this: "How dare you speak my mother's name, have a drawing of her hanging on your wall and yet not give me the information that I have requested. I have a right to know ..." but she kept her feelings bottled up, because by hook or by crook she knew she would get to the bottom of this mystery.

David sensed her anger and reached out and held her hand, just for a second and mouthed the words, "It's okay; we'll find out." Together they would get the answers they needed.

"Professor Lambert, I wonder if you might be so kind as to explain to us," David cleared his throat to ask his question, "where we are and ... how we came to be here?"

Bobby felt secretly pleased that David was able to talk the professor's language. Clearly they had been brought up in similar environments.

"Ah yes, the matter of time travel," the professor said thoughtfully. "Well now, let me see, how best to explain this?" he tapped the side of his head.

"Have you ever heard of space-time continuums, parallel universes and dimensions, time travel machines or of Oracles for that matter?"

"Well yes, I have actually. But in our reality they are things that have only been written about in books. They're not actually something that anyone has ever succeeded in inventing, well not to my knowledge, anyway."

"Well, what if I told you that what you have been reading in books is actually a possibility? What if I told you that people in your time have actually had the ability to do this kind of travel for a very long time? Hard to believe, I know. But how else do you explain all of this?" he asked with his eyes widened and again he gestured with his arm in a 180 degree arc. "What if people in your time could do these things and then kept it secret for fear of the top minds of the world and governments catching on and then disturbing the natural balance of things and so destroying the immense beauty of this paradise of which you have already been witness to." He now had the children's full attention. Finally they were getting the information they'd been asking for.

He went to a massive chalkboard and drew a long white line with chalk. He then proceeded to write the years along the line starting from the beginning of time and reaching all the way into the future jumping between the ages every 1000 or 1,000,000 years or so. He then drew another line above this one and on it wrote unusual words that the children had never heard of — perhaps it was a different language.

"Now, bear with me if you will. Just imagine that there exists the ability to go from here," he pointed to 1930, which was almost at the end of the first line, "to here," and he pointed to another spot on the second line right back at the beginning where he had written the word "Gufawemici".

"Roughly translated this means 'Garden of Eden,'" he said pointing to the unusual word. The children looked at one another in astonishment. Of course, it made perfect sense ... what other place could this be? The professor went on to explain a lot of other things in a very scientific fashion which both of the children had difficulty understanding.

Besides, they were both immersed in their own thoughts and each of them was wondering how it was that they had been the ones chosen to come to this living and breathing Garden of Eden.

"Oh, not just you, my lovelies," the professor said,

cutting into their thoughts making each of them feel as if he had read their minds yet again.

"No, not just you, but your ancestors too!"

"Excuse me," David said.

"Let me put it this way. Back in 1930 your time, a bunch of bedraggled, boisterous and bored children found the crystal ball that you have in your backpack, Bobby — a story that can wait for another time — and after reading the fancy print on the ball — Oracle in the Mist — the children found themselves involved in an enormous adventure. They each had an idea in their minds of where they hoped they would end up but because they were not aware that they themselves had the powers to manifest a destination within them and because they were all completely terrified of what the outcome would be, their worst fears came true.

"I hate to be the one to have to tell you this but your ancestors Ina and Henry, landed themselves and six other youngsters in a dark and sinister place that they would later refer to as the 'workhouse'." Bobby and David stared wide-eyed at the professor and each of them was positively bursting with questions to ask the professor. Especially David who was wondering why the professor was referring to the other children as their "ancestors". But they were also intensely curious to find out what had happened to the original eight.

"Please continue," David said, enthusiastically.

"With pleasure," said the professor rubbing his hands

together with delight. He gave a slight bow and then proceeded to make another pot of tea. "Good things shouldn't be rushed," he added. The children sensed that this story was going to take some time to tell.

Chapter 9
THE EVIL ORACLE

"The children had no idea that the crystal ball that they had found actually belonged to an evil Oracle that lived in an even eviller land," the professor continued, now that he had made some more tea and resumed his position next to the children.

⤔ And so his story began ⤏

This evil Oracle was actually the one who had lured the children into the oak tree on the Brewsters' property. Oh, she wanted the children all right; she intended to put them to work in her workhouse but most of all she wanted her crystal ball back. She had lost it thousands of years earlier (she was very old, you know) and since that day was unable to have another crafted that was just like it. All attempts failed, much to the Oracle's fury. Many innocent craftspeople were murdered and thrown into her furnaces for failing her. She felt that losing the ball had weakened her power and power was the one

Oracle in the Mist   **85**

thing that the evil Oracle lived for. In fact it was what kept her alive. With a soul as black as night, the Oracle fed on the screams and sorrows of the poor, innocent children she had kidnapped over the years and the faster and more cruelly they died, the more powerful she became. She would never give up on her quest to find the ball.

On waking up after stepping into the tree the children found themselves in a huge wooden dormitory. There were slits in between the slats of wood on the walls so that freezing draughts blew into the dormitory and the ceiling was completely covered in spiders' webs and huge spiders darted in and out of them menacing the children as if threatening to come and take them at any minute. The children found themselves lying on filthy, mouldy mattresses and they could hear machines being operated in the room next door and a taunting voice that sang a sinister song over and over again:

"Don't ever make a creak,
Don't ever make a sound,
All does not move in
The house in New–Found.

Eryting is still,
Eryting is quiet,
To wake up herself is

To perish in the fire.

Keep your head down,
Keep your hands working,
The shadows are watching,
In corners they're lurking.

Don't ask for more food,
Don't whinge that you're cold,
Herself will just kill you,
For being so bold.

The children had quite by accident stumbled into the foul dungeons of dread that belonged to the Oracle. She had lured them to her place of residence in order to get her ball back.

In front of the beds that the children found themselves in, were many rows of windows that opened up outwards and upwards. Henry turned the latch of one of the windows and opened it to see what was making that awful sound. They all jumped up to go and peer through the opened window. On the other side of the window was a vast factory of massive machines the likes of which the children had never seen before.

They were huge, reaching up to the immense ceiling and were covered in knobs and handles and had large openings that things were fed into.

Henry, who was a farm boy and so knew about all kinds of machinery, looked at the machines but was puzzled. As far as he could see they made no sense. Things were being fed into them all right but nothing then came out the other side. All at once the children noticed the ugly creatures that seemed to run the place — judging by the keys they wore around their necks and the batons and whips they held in their hands. They were what the children had heard referred to as 'orcs' from the stories they had read in the past. But even worse than all of that was the appalling state of the children who operated the machines. They looked as though they hadn't eaten a decent meal or had a shower in months and their clothes were all in tatters. Worse still was the look of fear they all had on their faces as they watched the other children being whipped and tortured if they so much as sneezed. It seemed as if at any given moment these poor children would be gobbled up by one of those huge machines ...

"What's this then?" one of the orcs demanded of a little boy no older than six.

"I'm sorry sir, but it's just that I'm so tired and me hands can't keep up with the pace sir, and ..."

"Not good enough though is it me lad? In wiv ya then!" And with that he picked up the little boy with one hand, and to the cries of sheer terror from the boy and all of the other children, threw him head first into the jaws of the machine. Blood spurted everywhere and the sound of bones being crunched reverberated throughout the factory and reached the eight new arrivals behind the opened window.

"Oh my God, did I just see what I think I saw?" Ina said to Henry and all of the younger children who had seen the incident either started to cry or buried their heads into Henry and Ina's shoulders in fear.

"Where on earth have we ended up?" Henry looked at Ina, terrified as well. "Have we stumbled into a hell for children?"

"What's all this noise?"

The children heard a female voice that was hissing and cruel. Then they heard a sliding, slithering sound and watched as a strange creature that seemed to have tentacles instead of legs, but also wore a dress, came into their view.

She left a trail of slime behind her as she progressed to the centre of the factory. The children all fell quiet at once to listen to what the creature was about to say.

Henry told the children to be quiet but it was too late. The boss creature had spotted them peering through the window and recognised them at once.

"There they are," she cried pointing towards the children. "They have my ball. Well, don't just stand there; go and get them and bring them to me and don't lose or damage my precious crystal ball or it will be into the furnace with you." All of the orc-looking creatures immediately started to head towards the exit that led to the dormitory.

The children all started to scream and cry in terror but luckily Henry had a plan. He had noticed a large window that led out on the roof tops of the adjoining factories.

Since the window was locked he took a chair and smashed at the window until it shattered. He then took the children and one by one led them out onto the roof — only just in time too because the orcs were not afraid of heights and were not afraid to chase them across the rooftops.

Henry finally found a ladder that they could scramble down to safety on the path. The children were most alarmed to find that the whole town seemed made up of these kind of orcs and all sorts of other creatures too, all evil and foul smelling. Some of them looked around in alarm and decided to give chase even though they had no idea why they were chasing the children. But most of them just grunted at the mob of children running past. Before they knew it the children found themselves on the docks of a vast ocean and Henry realised that the only way the children were going to get away from this foul place was to jump aboard a ship. The one that Henry chose just happened to be having her rope untied as the children boarded and luckily for the children, orcs just happen to be incredibly short-sighted and all of the crew were too busy with their individual duties to notice a group of mainly small children whisk past them faster than a hare and out of sight into the kitchen of the giant ship.

The workhouse orcs made it to the dock just as the ship was pulling out and Henry could hear shouts of "Hey, you there, did ya see a bunch of kids who are not from around 'ere?"

"What?" came the confused reply.

"Kids, you know — about eight of 'em. We can't find 'em."

But the ship was pulling out at full steam and already there was some distance between the orcs on the ship and the orcs on the dock.

"Nah, we don't want no kids. What would we want kids for?" The orc on the ship had completely misunderstood the workhouse orc's question.

"I know, but 'ave ya seen any, like?" the orc on the dock persisted.

"Look mate, you must be in the wrong place 'cause I ain't seen no ..." but just then and not a moment too soon, a huge wind blew up and his voice was carried off with it into the distance."

"What ya sayin'?" said the orc on the dock, but would you believe the ship's horn blew and was so loud that the wood on the dock actually vibrated under the workhouse orc's feet? Eventually they both gave up trying to have the conversation at all and the orc on the dock turned and ran off to the rest of the other orcs and they ran back towards the workhouse. The ship drew up her anchor and set off out to sea.

The children hid themselves away in the galley of the boat. They found an excellent place to hide behind huge sacks of flour, potatoes and piles of tins of beans and sardines.

Henry looked around and was pleased with the fact that they would have something to eat. The trick now was not getting caught. Every time the orc cook came in to get a new ingredient the children had to make sure they were out of sight. It wasn't long though until the orcs had finished with the kitchen for the night and the children could relax a little and make a meal for themselves.

After a simple, cold meal the children sat around and told stories of what their favourite destinations would be. Going home, of course rated on top of the list. It seemed to relax the younger children to talk of such things and Henry and Ina liked that their imaginations were still alive with adventure.

It was the general consensus that given a choice the children would choose a beautiful, deserted island as their ideal destination. The way they described it made it sound like a regular Garden of Eden, complete with every animal that ever lived throughout the millennium and of course no evil lurking in corners and danger for them to have to worry about. They would have the whole island to themselves and have plenty of fresh food to eat and lovely fish to catch from the ocean.

The younger children fell asleep on the laps of Henry and Ina and were soon breathing deeply. What a big day they had had. After a while Ina looked at Henry and asked, "Have you realised what I've realised, Henry?"

"What do you mean?" he whispered back. "Is it about the fact that we no longer have a way home because there's no Oracle to guide us through the crystal ball?"

"Yes, that's exactly what I'm talking about. What are we going to do?"

"Look, tomorrow's a new day and we'll find a way out of this. Don't you worry about that Ina." He could see that she was very frightened.

"Now, do me a favour and go to sleep will you Ina? I'm going to need you to be at your strongest tomorrow. Who knows what's in store for us then?"

Luckily Ina didn't argue with Henry and she didn't ask him any more questions that he just couldn't answer.

He smiled warmly at her and watched as she drifted into a fretful sleep with a worried frown on her face. He may have been smiling but inside he was frozen with anxiety and fear. He turned the question over in his mind too many times to remember during the course of the night, not allowing himself to fall asleep for fear of being discovered by the orcs: how to get out of this rotten place and back home where they belonged? He regretted deeply ever allowing the other children to convince him to take part in this stupid plan. He was now responsible for all of their lives being the eldest and the burden was almost too much to bear. 'What would Dad do in this position?' he asked himself and he heard his father's voice in his head saying: "Never mind sonny Jim.There, there. No point crying over spilt milk. What's done is done mate. Just have to soldier on and remember that tomorrow's a brand new day with brand new adventures." This comforted Henry somewhat and helped him to drift into a shallow sleep even if it was with one eye open.

The children awoke with a start at first light to the sound of, "Eh, what's this then?" being shouted by the head cook who had come into the pantry to fetch breakfast ingredients.

Luckily Henry was thinking quickly. He stood up and hit the cook, knocking him unconscious before he had the chance to say anything else. But it was too late. The children heard the sounds of orcs banging and thumping about and footsteps scuttling towards them from the other side of the ship.

"Quick," Henry shouted at the others. "There's no time to lose," and they scrambled up the ladder to escape the orcs once again. The morning sun hit their eyes and almost blinded them but after a moment Henry could see a life raft complete with oars on the side of the ship.

He wasted no time, hurled it into the water and then sent Ina down the ladder followed by each of the other children until they were all safely bobbing about in the tiny boat on the ocean swell. The orcs reached him just as he was about to descend down the ladder and so he jumped into the ocean beside the raft and then quickly scrambled into it and grabbing the oars, began to steer the little boat away from the ship.

"Eh, come back 'ere you kids. Who are you anyway and how did you get on my boat? Get back here. You can't take my life raft ..." and with that he pushed one of the grunts over the edge of the ship and said, "Go on, go and get 'em and bring 'em back."

"Yes sir, shall do Captain," said the orc from the water, and everyone watched as he dog-paddled in the water but did not swim.

"Eh, don't tell me you can't swim? Oh flipperty

jibbert, just my luck! Who here can swim, then?" he demanded of his crew and all of them looked downcast as if embarrassed to admit it.

"So, what, we jus' gonna let those kids get away?" he screamed at his crew, "I don' believe this."

"Why don' you jump in then, Captain?" came a voice from the crowd.

"Who said that, who said that then? I'll find out who you are and I swear by the time I'm through with you ..." and he held up his fist in a fury at the crowd.

The children could hear all of this as they rowed away and they couldn't help having a little giggle to themselves, especially when it became clear that not one of the orcs could swim and chase them. They began to feel sure that they would indeed escape.

"I'm sorry, Captain," Henry shouted back across the swell. "I'll have you know that I'm not a thief but this is the only option available to me."

All of the orcs looked at one another and shrugged their shoulders, including the captain. The children could see that they could not hear what Henry had said at all. There was too much distance between them now, but at least Henry had done the right thing and apologised.

It wasn't long and the ship was a blur in the distance behind them. The children became mesmerised by the ship and could still see the orcs just standing there on the deck, as if in disbelief at what had just happened. But then the ship disappeared from view behind the swell and the children's attention came back to the fact that they were adrift in an unknown ocean and heading to goodness knows where with no water and food.

"This is the best adventure that I've ever had," said Johnny, who was nine and was always talking about wanting to travel the world, having fun and fighting pirates and dragons and finding buried treasures. "Do you think we'll see pirates soon?" was his next question.

"Well, what do you think those were?" answered Teresa who was six and very sensible and thought that wanting to have adventures was very silly and boyish.

"Ina, I'm thirsty and hungry," Teresa said and looked about herself in the raft and in the ocean. Not much chance of anything to eat or drink out here. All of the rest of the children remained quiet but they stared at Henry and Ina with big, questioning eyes.

"Now, don't worry," answered Ina, "because we're going to be all right. We've been all right so far, haven't we? And we're going to keep being all right but you have to be patient."

Right at that moment, Johnny, who had been standing up at the end of the raft with his hands joined together and curled over to form a pretend eyeglass to look towards the horizon, shouted, "Hey, is that land I see over there, Henry?" All of the children craned their necks in the direction that he had pointed and squinted into the bright sunlight.

"Good lord," said Henry, "I believe he's right. Good spotting Johnny," and he turned the raft around and started to head towards the land on the horizon.

"Land ahoy, land ahoy," the children all squealed with delight, for once able to imitate the famous line from the many children's stories that had been read to them.

"Can I take over with the rowing for a while?" asked Ina, wanting to be of help.

"No, that's fine, I've got it," answered Henry.

It's true; he is quite capable, Ina thought to herself. He'd been rowing for all of this time and yet he didn't seem even a little tired. Ina marvelled at Henry's strength. Being born and raised on a farm where even the toddlers were expected to help with the chores Henry had become a very lean, strong and capable fourteen-year-old boy. Ina felt puny and weak in contrast to Henry. She thought about her own upbringing. She had never had to worry about chores as there were always servants to do everything and she only had her studies, piano lessons, her horse and tea parties with friends to think about. She had to admit, even though she didn't like boys in general, she quite admired Henry.

It wasn't long before the land became bigger and bigger as the children drew closer. They became quite excited, all except for Ina who was worried that there might be danger lurking on the island. But then, it wasn't long before even she became swept up in their enthusiasm as well. She hoped that there would be food and water available for them.

Before long they were on the shores of what seemed to be a beautiful, tropical island, not unlike the one they had talked about the night before. They disembarked in the shallows and helped Henry to pull the raft up on to the sand. They stood there in a little huddle, staring about when all of a sudden a huge lion came out of the forest and walked towards them. Henry ordered all of them back into the raft and he grabbed an oar to defend himself. All of the children sat holding their breath as the lion walked towards them. Ina felt as if her heart had dropped into her stomach but at the same time she had an incredible feeling of peace, as if there was really nothing to worry about at all.

The lion got within six feet of Henry and then stood quite still and let out an almighty, ear-splitting roar.

It then nodded its head up and down as if to

convey some kind of message and with that turned and walked back into the forest.

"Do you believe it?" shouted Johnny. "Oh my God, I've never seen anything like that before. This must be some kind of magical land where everything is friendly and nothing can ..."

Right then came a blood curdling cry from Teresa and she sat pointing to the jungle. The children all looked to where she was pointing only to see the most incredible spectacle, one which almost defied description. They all drew in their breath sharply and stared at one another in utter amazement.

There before them were all manner of animals and other creatures too — the likes of which they'd never seen before but looking most prehistoric — all coming out of the forest and wandering about totally oblivious to the children as if all going on their hurried way to previous engagements.

The children stood and sat, mouths agape at the picture before them. Not one of them uttered a word. And then an even more peculiar thing happened. A monkey came bounding out of the forest and came right up to them and said, "Orr, orr, orr, screech." Ina and Henry looked at each other blankly. Clearly the monkey was trying to say something to them but they had no idea what.

"Orr, orr, orr, screech," it repeated, but this time

he took a few steps towards the forest and then turned back to them and motioned to them, as if they should follow him. Then he did the same thing again and nodded his head as if to say, it's okay, you can follow me.

"Well, I don't see that we have any choice but to follow him, do you?" Henry asked Ina. Ina was too shocked to answer. She looked at him blankly and shrugged her shoulders. Meanwhile Johnny was already off and running and calling to them all, "Come on. He's going to get us something to eat and drink," as if that was their most important priority.

"How do you know that? Come back! It's too dangerous," Henry shouted to him.

"I don't know," answered Johnny, "I just know somehow that it's okay."

Ina took Teresa's hand in hers and altogether the children made their way to the forest. Snakes slithered by as they walked along and spiders scurried about too, which made all of the children give little shouts of surprise each time but after a while, once the children realised that the creatures meant them no harm they stopped even noticing their presence.

"I feel as though I'm dreaming," Ina said to Henry as they walked along. "It's too bizarre to be true. It's almost as if what we talked about last night has come true."

"I know," answered Henry shaking his head. "If that's the case, then there will be fresh food and drinking water here and we'll come to no harm."

"Yes, I suppose," Ina agreed.

Off into the distance the children could hear a waterfall cascading. That would be their fresh water. The monkey took them along a narrow, sandy path and through a lush fern glade that had a carpet of soft moss underfoot. And then they began to climb up tiny stairs that eventually led to a plateau on which they found themselves standing under a massive house held up by bamboo stilts.

"Orr, orr, orr, screech," said the monkey and pointed behind them. They all turned at the same time and what they saw completely took their breath away. Ina and Henry lifted the younger ones so that they could see. A sparkling ocean with every sea creature imaginable and also unimagined, playing about in the ocean and a sky full of birds of all descriptions, even a prehistoric variety just playing about in the sky, as if floating on the breeze.

"It's just like in my dream," said Teresa. "This is what we talked about last night and this is what I dreamed about during the night too." She was very excited.

Ina looked at Henry who just looked puzzled. He

was looking behind them and then pointing to the left of them as if trying to ascertain which direction they were facing.

"I can't understand how we didn't see all of this when we were out on the ocean," he said to Ina.

"Well, we must have been on the other side of the island," she answered.

"Yes, but ..."

The monkey spoke to them again and they began their ascent to the house. On entering the house the children found a spotlessly clean, open plan and scarcely furnished inside area. The kitchen was fully stocked with all kinds of foods that they would normally enjoy at home. There were freshly grown corn still in their husks, eggs, cheese, home-made bread, biscuits and cakes, lettuces, tomatoes, cucumbers, and lovely looking freshly caught salmon.

The children started to salivate just looking at all of the delicious food. Ina set about preparing a meal for them all and it wasn't long before they were all sitting down and eating to their hearts' content and taking in the lovely view from the window looking out over the forest and to the ocean. It really was like a dream come true.

Luckily the children hadn't realised that they were being watched by the natives of the island, a gentle and yet fierce people who wished to remain anonymous and hidden away from their view. For a very long time, only the animals knew of their existence.

Chapter 10
HENRY, INA AND THE ISLAND PARADISE

T he children found the accommodation within the lodge quite comfortable. They were able to bed down the boys on one side of the lodge and the girls on the other with a curtain drawn between them so they all had some privacy. It felt most peculiar at first to be away from their homes and parents and little Teresa and some of the other young children complained fearfully at first about missing their mothers, fathers, favourite teddies and dollies or brothers and sisters. Henry and Ina had to gently explain to the younger children that they would have returned home if they could but that it was impossible. The children wept bitterly at first but after a time they came to accept their new surroundings and before long they thought of it as home.

Gradually the days slipped into weeks and then the weeks into months and the children became accustomed to the island and its strange inhabitants. No day was ever without an

Oracle in the Mist   **105**

adventure as the children made friends with all of the island's animals and taught themselves skills such as how to catch fish with a home-made spear from the sea and recognising which berries could be eaten and would taste delicious and sweet.

None of them questioned the fact that every now and then a donkey would appear from nowhere laden with provisions for them that would last some weeks.

After a while, all of the children, even Henry, stopped questioning every little miracle that occurred.

Johnny developed a talent for communicating with the animals. It wasn't in any obvious, verbal way but he always seemed to know the message they were trying to convey and he would talk to them in his own plain English and somehow a link was established between them.

The island was a place of good tidings and the children found that they never had to worry about sickness, not even a sniffle or injuries or accidents. In fact they didn't even have to worry about becoming too hot or too cold either. The days were warm and balmy and the nights were pleasantly cool. It really was the ideal location.

A close bond formed between all of the children

and eventually it was as if the children were a family with familial ties.

Henry and Ina became the natural leaders of the group and it was obvious that there was a great affection between them for on this island all of the differences of their upbringing faded into insignificance.

The months became years and the children had almost completely forgotten about their other lives. Henry celebrated his twentieth birthday and Ina her nineteenth birthday when something most extraordinary happened.

A native man with extremely dark skin appeared out of nowhere and spoke to the children in their own language. "Welcome to our island, we would like to meet all of you. The leader of my tribe wishes for you to come tonight to our celebrations and also wishes for you to know that you will come to no harm," and with that he thumped himself hard on his own chest and disappeared the same magical way that he had come.

"I can't believe we didn't know they were here all of this time," Ina said to Henry.

"This is incredible," Henry agreed. "That must be where all of the food's been coming from all of these years. How have they remained hidden for all of this time?"

"Maybe we haven't been here for that long at all," said Johnny and they all looked at him incredulously.

"Well, you heard him. He said, 'Welcome to the island.' To him we only just got here," Johnny made a very valid point.

"What are we going to do?" asked Ina, not feeling very sure about meeting the whole tribe.

"Well, I don't see that we have any choice but to go," answered Henry, logical as always. "If nothing else we have to go and thank them for sharing their food and this island with us for all of these years."

Ina could see that Henry was convinced and she knew him well enough to know that there was no point trying to change his mind. Her mind immediately went to the appalling state of their clothing. They had all outgrown their one set of clothes each and so had fashioned them into comfortable attire by cutting the legs off pants and sleeves off jumpers and shirts.

All of their clothes were in tatters and very stained and stiff and faded like old cardboard due to being washed in sea water for so long. Oh well, the natives would just have to accept them even though they looked so bedraggled.

That night the children made their way to meet the tribe as the man had returned to show them the way. The most astonishing thing about all of this was the fact that an entire village of natives existed right here where all of the children had been playing and frolicking for many years. It was as if a veil, which had now come down, had existed between the children's and the natives' world. But the children didn't question it because by now they were used to all kinds of strange things happening.

The elder of the tribe turned out to be an old toothless crone who was wearing virtually nothing and was shrunken with age and covered in necklaces of animal teeth. She was very much revered by the other natives. What she said was obeyed and the crowds parted so that she could come forth.

"Henry and Ina?" she said when she saw them and she pointed her stick made of an old bone at them.

"Yes, that's right," they said in unison.

"What do you think?" she asked, using her stick to swirl around her as if referring to the island.

"Excuse me?" asked Henry.

"I say, what do you think, child? Do you like what you have created?" she asked, smiling at them.

Henry and Ina looked at one another puzzled.

"Oh, do you mean the island?" answered Ina, "Oh yes, we really do like living here and thank you so much for giving us all of that food all through the years and I'm terribly sorry for the way we look. We haven't been able to locate more clothes …"

"Clothes don't matter because now you wear what we wear. You came recently, did you know that?" the old Crone was still smiling at them as if she was the keeper of some incredible secret of which they had no idea. But, by now the children were used to feeling this way, as if they were living through some kind of constant mysterious miracle that always had them in a state of continual obliviousness, with all questions remaining unanswered.

They had felt this way for so many years now that they had almost forgotten how to feel any other way.

"And now, we join you together," said the Crone and she stepped forward and took the hands of Henry and Ina and placed them together. She started to laugh.

"What?" spluttered Ina, "Join us together? Oh no, you can't do that! What do you mean? You don't understand — where we come from you need a priest to perform a task such as that and besides we can't do something like that because where we come from, we're actually quite young, aren't we Henry?" she said looking over to Henry. But for some strange reason he was smiling as well as if he had already known of the Crone's plan and he took her hand firmly in his and stared deeply into her eyes in the most loving way.

Before Ina knew what was happening or could

protest at all, a bunch of beautiful, young native women came and took her hand and led her to a hut. She looked back and was about to ask Henry to rescue her but found that he was being led into another hut by a group of young men.

Ina talked incessantly to the young women who were dressing her as she really was quite nervous about what was about to take place. Were they talking about a marriage?

Surely she'd misunderstood. The women tore at the scant clothes that she wore. They seemed to have no idea of modesty and she cried out several times and attempted to cover herself back up again. They ignored her and replaced her clothes with a costume more like their own: a long grass skirt and a long piece of fabric wrapped around her bosom in the fashion of a bikini. They put up her long, frizzy hair with shell combs and painted her face with ochre to make it look more like theirs. They layered jewels and draped exquisite-looking fabric around her shoulders and arms.

It soon became evident that they were preparing her for something quite special as by the end of it all, her outfit was far more elaborate than any of theirs. They left her feet bare.

When she was taken out of the hut, she came face to face with Henry, who had also been done up in the native attire. All of her nervousness melted away when they locked eyes and they giggled and pointed at one another like little children. The other children took one look at them and laughed uproariously. The Crone took Henry and Ina by their hands and led them to a place under an arbour made of tropical flowers. She put their hands together and stood before them.

"Ina, I know you love this man, yes?" she asked.

Ina looked at Henry and started to blush. They had never spoken of their feelings for one another prior to this but before Ina could stop herself she heard herself say, "Yes, I do."

"And Henry, I know you love this woman, yes?"

"Yes, I do," he answered.

Both Ina and Henry could hear the children giggling and saying all kinds of things behind them such as "Lovebirds" and "Ooh Henry loves Ina" and so on pretending to taunt them. But Henry and Ina took no offence. They were too busy grinning madly at each other.

"Yes, that's good, because now Henry you are going to be the husband of this young Ina. You are not children anymore and it is now time to become as one. So, as the elder of this tribe I ask you, will you always love one another and stand by one another no matter what problems you have and will you always be there for one another?"

"I will," they both said in unison, their smiles going from ear to ear.

"That's good, because now you are man and wife and you can have a kiss," the Crone said.

Henry took Ina's shoulders and pulled her closer to him and they kissed lightly and then turned to look at the children who were all saying things like: "Oooh, kissy, kissy, smooch, smooch" and kissing the backs of their own hands and making squeaking sounds, to fully stir up the occasion.

"Good," said the Crone, "now we have the party. I love parties."

All of the children were taken to another area of the village where they came upon massive tables all fully laden with a banquet of delicious-looking food. They all ate and then the natives entertained them by playing drums and singing and dancing in their own fashion. They insisted that the children join in on the fun and so by the end of the night all of the children had learnt a new form of dance. They couldn't remember the last time they'd had this much fun. At around midnight the old Crone came to Henry and Ina and putting their hands together once more said, "And now it is time ..." and she lead them away to a lone hut on the edge of the village and motioned for them to go inside and then she closed the door. "See you in the morning, husband and wife," she said with a hearty laugh.

The rest of the children were taken back to the house on stilts and slept there without Henry and Ina for the first time since coming to the island.

The next day all of the children were given the clothing of the natives and the natives started to teach the children their own ways. It wasn't long before all of the people became united as one, spending all of their time together and learning each other's customs.

After some time, it became evident that Ina would have a baby. Everyone was thrilled about it. The thought of having another little baby on the island to play with the native children made them very happy. Ina was happy as well but she was also concerned. She spoke to the Crone about the fact that she had no one there to help her birth the baby.

She didn't have the slightest notion of such things and the thought of it made her frightened. But the Crone told her not to worry. "It's the most natural thing in the world Ina, don't be worried. You'll be fine. I will have women helping you who have delivered dozens of babies. Look at all of our lovely children here. There's nothing wrong with them, is there?"

That was true, Ina thought to herself. The children of the natives really were most adorable and they all had mothers that had obviously survived the births. It was probably nothing to worry about but still, she couldn't help wishing to herself that she would have her very own private doctor.

Within a few days of making her wish, it was granted. An Englishman by the name of Professor Lambert strolled into the village, quite by magic of course and looking as if nothing out of the ordinary had happened.

"Obstetrics is my qualification but you know, I have to say that I really rather like the idea of being a botanist. That's where my special interest lies. Still, at your service I am, Ina Fairweather. And have no fear, I have delivered many babies and never had a problem with one."

Ina was so relieved to hear this and it was lovely to have another person come to the island. He was able to teach the children about many things to do with plant life and even knew a lot about the animals as well. But when asked from where he had come, a cloud would come over his face.

"Well, you know, I'm really quite embarrassed to say this but I have absolutely no idea. I know that I've read a great many books but I don't know where they are. I remember conversations that I've had with colleagues and that my father was a most refined and learned gentleman but I don't know where in the world he is or where I was before coming to this island. I have to tell you, I'm just as alarmed as you are at my sudden appearance here and yet I'm very happy to be able to offer my assistance and I know that in time the explanation we are all looking for will come to light. We just have to be patient."

Ina thought him to be a very nice person to be so accepting of being taken from his own world and placed here and she was very grateful at having a qualified doctor in her midst, especially now that there was a baby coming.

When Ina's time came to have the baby, the doctor and native midwives were all prepared and before they knew it they were all celebrating the birth of a healthy baby boy. Henry and Ina were ecstatic with the safe arrival of their baby and thanked the professor profusely. Henry didn't leave the side of his wife and baby for some days.

Chapter 11

THE EIGHT RETURN HOME

A bout a month after the birth of the baby, the Crone asked Henry for more information as to how they came to be living on the island. When Henry spoke of the crystal ball she asked to see it and then for some mysterious reason she took the ball and disappeared with it for some days. On her return she called a meeting asking every single person and even some of the animals to attend.

"A matter of importance has come to my attention and that is why I am calling this meeting," she began with a grave look on her face.

"I am not sure if this is good news or not but I have just discovered a way to send all of the children back to their home ... back to the other time dimension that is so far from here," she said and she waved her hand into the air.

All of the children looked to one another in shock. Could this really be true? They'd all but forgotten that other place, the place they once called home.

"My dear children," she continued, "I can see that

now is the time to make a very important decision, one that I cannot make for you. Only you can decide the right thing to do."

The children all looked from one to another but it was Teresa who broke the silence.

"So does that mean I would get to see my mummy again?" she asked.

"Yes," said Ina, clutching onto her baby tightly. Something told her that things would not, could not be the same for her and Henry once back in the other world. She felt frightened.

Henry looked at her and their baby and smiled but then spoke logically as only he could, to everyone gathered, "Even though we've come to love this island and consider it our home it is the honourable thing to do to go back home and at least see our parents and loved ones and let them know we are all right. After that, if we still feel the same we can come back here to live. But in the meantime we really do owe it to our parents to let them know we are all alive and well and healthy."

"But Henry," Ina asked, "how are we going to explain this?" and she pointed to their baby.

"Well, let's not worry about that Ina. We'll just explain everything and if they can't accept it then we'll just come back here to live."

Ina knew that what Henry said sounded viable enough but her instinct told her that it was not going to be that easy. Nevertheless over the course of the next few days she became swept up in the excitement of returning home and convinced herself that there was nothing to worry about. After all, what could possibly go wrong?

The old Crone had found a tropical version of the giant old oak tree, complete with a hole large enough to fit all eight children. The children said their goodbyes and entered the tree and the Crone spoke a few magical words and then handed the ball back to Ina before, just as happened last time, the children vanished from sight under a canopy of lightning and flashing lights.

Within what seemed like seconds the children were lying in their beds safely back in their homes. Each child was met with varying degrees of shock and surprise as parents and brothers and sisters greeted the child that they had almost given up for dead.

Even more shocking than their return home was the fact that not one of the children could remember where they had been or what had kept them away from home for so long. They each awoke in exactly the same state, including the same clothes that they had been in when they had disappeared six days earlier. Ina implored her mother to please stop asking her questions to which she had no idea of the answers. All she knew was that she was a thirteen-year-old girl who felt as if her heart was breaking but she had no idea why. It was as if there was something missing ...

The next day the whole town gathered to talk about what should be done about the incident. Ina and Henry caught each other's eye and stared at one another shyly. Something passed between them. It was also obvious to Ina's mother, who took Ina to the opposite side of the hall away from the boy. She would not have a boy staring at her daughter in that manner.

Then the group had their photograph taken and were asked several questions by the local newspaper reporters to which all of the children answered, "I don't know, I don't know," until eventually the reporters gave up and went away. Then the local police wanted questions answered too but when they saw that the children clearly had no memory of what had befallen them even they gave up and stopped asking questions. The whole town decided to just forget about the matter and to keep quiet about it for fear the whole world would come to stare at the children and treat them like circus freaks or some such thing. From then on it was referred to as the "1930 incident" but the parents of the children who had vanished were determined to protect their children and each and every one of them refused

Linda Maree Malcolm

to discuss the matter with even their own brothers, sisters or parents.

The whole town was also alarmed to find out that a baby had mysteriously appeared under the old oak out on the Brewsters' property. Celebrations were held in light of the fact that Doctor Game and his wife finally became the proud parents of a very healthy baby boy.

Ina noticed a lump in her bed and pulled out the crystal ball. How odd, she thought. She had no recollection as to how it came to be there but her instincts told her that all of these events were connected and that her mother would be so angry if she was to find it. She cut out all of the newspaper articles that related to the incident and taping them together hid them with the crystal ball in the attic, a place she was sure no-one else would ever go. She knew she must never let on about its existence but still couldn't help feeling that maybe one day she might just need it for something and so in the meantime it would have to be her very own secret.

Chapter 12
COUSINS

D avid and Bobby were riveted to the spot the whole time the professor was telling his story. They both shook their heads in disbelief, not even knowing which question to ask first.

"So, let me get this right," David finally found his voice. "This island is the result of a wish or a manifestation, as you call it, dreamed up by a whole bunch of kids 80 years ago? They simply visualised the very existence they wished to have?"

"Correct," answered the professor. "Think of it as a kind of holographic image, a window from your world into another — a complete dimension in its own right, living separately but beside your world, as you know it.

The concept of manifestation and visualisation wasn't a foreign one to Bobby. In fact she'd manifested all kinds of things in the past like books or a new outfit or shoes but the thought of manifesting an entire island was beyond her.

"It can't be ..." David spoke her thoughts as well. "And how is it that the children spent six years here and yet only six days passed by the time they had returned back to our world? I just don't understand."

"Ah yes, good question. Well, you see each day in your world is equivalent to one year here. But, and this is the interesting part, the children went back to their original ages on leaving here but if they had returned, experience has shown us, they would have returned here the same age as when they left us."

"I'm afraid I don't understand," David said truthfully.

"It's simple really," the professor said. "If, for example, Ina had returned here, she would have gone from being a girl of twelve back to being a young lady of eighteen and then when she returned to your world again she would return back to her original age of twelve."

"But how do you know that?" Bobby asked. "You must have had one or more of the original eight return here at some point.

"Oh yes. Well, that's another story for another day, don't you think?"

Bobby could feel that old feeling of frustration rising within her again. She made a mental note to herself again. There were two questions she would have to remember to ask at a later date now.

"And something else I've been curious about Professor?" asked David. "How did you know our names?"

"Ah yes, well that's all thanks to the native Oracle, the one that Henry and Ina called the Crone. She's a seer, actually and the night that Henry and Ina returned to your world she received information from the crystal ball that said the descendants of Ina and Henry, Bobby and David, would be here in the year 2010, which is your time and although a long time for people in your world, it is like a blink of an eye for us here. You see, here on this island there is no such thing as time."

David was still feeling extremely confused.

"But that doesn't make sense," he said puzzled. "I'm not a descendent of Henry and Ina. I'm the son of Doctor Game, who was the son of Doctor Game Senior.

"Yes, that is true, David," the professor said and his eyes softened towards David, "but surely you see that your father is not the biological son of your grandfather is he? Do you want to know who your biological grandfather is, David?"

"Yes, I do. In fact that's why I came on this quest. I've always wanted to know the answer to that. And I wanted to help Bobby of course."

"Well, it's Henry. The baby that Henry and Ina had here was somehow separated out of Ina's arms during the return trip and was found under the oak tree on the Brewsters' property and was then adopted by Dr Game. Do you see?" Bobby and David looked from one to another and then back to the professor in surprise.

"Of course," said David, "it all fits ... but if that's true then that means I'm the grandson of a farm boy not ... well, I just always assumed I came from a long line of doctors." He looked across to Bobby. "I'm aware that that sounds somewhat shallow."

"Look, it's a shock to get news like this," she comforted him. "Don't be too hard on yourself. At last you're starting to get answers anyway. So am I actually."

"I just want you to know David that your grandfather was a wonderful, caring man. He took care of all of those children as if they were his own and he was so young himself. He was someone you can be really proud of—"

Right at that moment there was a knock on the door and a tall, elegant native entered the house and announced, "It is time, Professor Lambert."

"Oh yes indeed, how excellent and just in the nick of time too. I've just finished telling the children about Ina and Henry. Now it's time to go and celebrate with the natives." He stood up and rubbing his hands together, ushered the children out of the house and back down the stairs again.

Before they knew it they were at the village again where there were many tables laid out with fine food, the likes of which the children had never seen before. It all looked very delicious. After they had eaten the children were taken to the beach where there was a massive, roaring bonfire.

Night began to fall and the natives started to play their instruments and sing and dance in exactly the same fashion as had been described to the children earlier by the professor. It was expected that David and Bobby would dance and sing too, which was quite a sight.

Suddenly all became quiet on the beach and the children became aware that something quite important was about to happen. The Oracle made her way onto the beach and was introduced to the children.

"Ah yes, Bobby and David, we have been waiting for you. I am glad you are here. I hope you are getting the answers to your questions and are feeling comfortable here. I brought you here because the evil workhouse Oracle whom Ina and Henry had to deal with all of those years ago has recently made her presence known to me." All of the natives, the professor and even Sebastian the monkey gasped and looked horror-stricken. Bobby and David looked at one another and David frowned. "Yes thank you, ah, I don't mean to be rude but what has that to do with us?" he asked.

"Yes, I see this is hard to understand but the workhouse Oracle insists that she has her crystal ball back and it's only a matter of time before she finds a way to this island. When she does all of this will be gone ... do you see? We are the creation of your ancestors and we can only continue to be if you both agree to help us."

"Yes, I do see," said David, "but unfortunately we have to make our way home to our own world and ..."

"I do understand," said Bobby interrupting David. "Just tell us what we have to do and we will do it." There was no way she would stand by and allow any harm to come to this beautiful place. David stared at her wide-eyed and disapproving. Here she goes again, he thought to himself. What is she getting us into this time? At that moment each child and the rest of the party became horrified as they witnessed the Oracle herself morph into a completely different creature right before their eyes. What they saw then was a massive figure, three metres tall, with a tiny head and tentacles for legs and wearing a tight fitting dress.

"Time to go home, my pets," it said with a mischievous hiss. "Don't be silly now. Give me back my ball and I'll send you home and then everyone's happy. Oh what a wonderful idea, don't you agree?" She was greeted with utter silence as they were all too shocked to answer, even the professor. Where was the old Crone anyway? Nothing like this had ever happened in the history of the island.

"Now, now, my pets," she warned louder and with more urgency, "don't mess with me. Just do what I say and you get to walk away with your lives, do you see? You don't want to make me angry, now. You might regret that, believe me."

"You don't frighten me," said Bobby, going right up to the face of the workhouse Oracle and pointing her finger at her. "I'm not giving you the ball or anything else for that matter so you might as well just go back to where you came from."

"Bobby," screamed David, "what are you doing? You're going to get us killed. Come back here."

"*You will regret this,*" the Oracle thundered at them and somehow she appeared even taller and larger than before. But Bobby didn't move an inch. She wouldn't back down to the Oracle. At that moment the Oracle disappeared and the native Crone was before them again. She looked very pale as if she was going to pass out, a look of shock and bewilderment on her face.

"She was here, wasn't she?" she asked, steadying herself by leaning on the professor. Everyone nodded their heads. "I knew it was just a matter of time. Her hold over me is getting stronger and stronger. Soon she will be able to shapeshift into my body for longer and longer periods of time and then she will have total control over all of this. And she won't stop until she gets her crystal ball back." She turned to Bobby and David to warn them. "I was wrong with what I said before, you both need to go home and away from here or your safety is in danger. Tomorrow you must go," she insisted. Bobby looked at David, not believing that he could just walk away from this. But the Crone was someone you didn't want to argue with.

"Okay," Bobby said, "but I will come back to help you. I'm the one with the ball and no-one can stop me from using it when I want." Bobby was determined to save the island and its inhabitants. David wasn't so keen, she could tell. He wouldn't talk about it with her. And even the professor said it was too dangerous for them to get involved in.

"But for now, let the festivities begin," said the Crone. The party started up again as if nothing had happened and the children were expected to take part as well. Finally, there were a few quiet moments where Bobby and David found themselves alone and able to talk to one another.

"What do you make of all this?" Bobby asked David.

"It's just incredible! I still can't really believe any of it. But I must admit I'm looking forward to going home tomorrow. What about you?"

"I can't believe you even want to go home, David Game. Why don't you want to stay and fight for the island?"

"You're impossible, Bobby," he said, slightly annoyed. "Don't you see what the situation is here? We're going to be killed and you don't really seem to care." She could see there was no persuading him but she knew that she would be back and that he couldn't stop her so she said nothing.

"Yes, well at least now I'm starting to understand what was really going on behind my grandmother's sad eyes. It's all starting to make more sense now, that's for sure."

"Yes, and just to think, I have the same ancestors as you! I just can't believe it." Bobby wasn't sure what David meant by this comment but she decided not to take offence at it.

"Yes and my grandmother is your grandmother which means ... oh my stars, David, do you realise what this means?"

"What, oh Lord, I hadn't thought of that ... you and I are cousins of sorts." They each shook their heads in disbelief.

"This is fabulous, David," Bobby said at last. "Do you know how long I've been wishing for a brother or sister or cousin or just any other kid to be related to by blood? I've always wanted to have a family, other than my mother, and have that feeling that I belong somewhere, and now I have that. I'll never forget this day, will you?" Bobby put both of her arms around David and laid her head on his shoulder. But for some reason he remained quite stiff and solemn-looking.

"What is it?" she asked.

"Oh, it's nothing really," he said but not very sincerely and gave her hand a quick rub. "Let's get back to the party, shall we?" He didn't want Bobby to know the real reason he felt completely crushed.

Bobby made a mental note to herself that she would have to find out what had really upset David. Maybe he didn't want a cousin. No, that can't be right, thought Bobby. Now she had three things she had to find out about. Anyhow, now that she knew he was her cousin she didn't feel quite as irritated by him. In fact she thought she might even be able to find it in herself to love him unconditionally, because that's what families do.

Bobby and David joined the party again, practising and getting quite good at the new dance they'd learnt. They did start to enjoy themselves in spite of the dangers and their difference of opinions. The festivities were held in their honour, after all. They were completely oblivious to the admiring stares of a thirteen-year-old native girl named Tinka who also just happened to be the princess of the tribe and her fourteen-year-old brother, Ranku, who was the prince. It was lucky actually that Bobby and David hadn't noticed Tinka and Ranku staring at them, with knowing smiles. The two native children were privy to a lot of secret information about Bobby and David and what was to come for them in their futures and the children may have found that slightly disconcerting.

Chapter 13

BOBBY AND DAVID COMPARE NOTES

The next morning the children awoke in the professor's house to a lovely home-cooked meal. Each of them was ready to greet the new day. Bobby thought about her mother Daphne but then she remembered that virtually no time had elapsed since leaving their world and so put the thought from her mind. Still, she felt eager to be on her way home now. During breakfast the professor told them of his plan to enable them to remember their adventure on getting home.

"So what I've done is written each of you a letter," he said and he produced two neatly folded letters with the children's names on them.

"You simply place the letter in your pocket and on returning home you will find it there and then on reading it you will be able to remember all of the details of your trip here. Okay then, best away." With that, the professor took the children to the same tree that was used 80 years earlier by the original eight children.

"Lovely to have finally met you," he said as they were

Oracle in the Mist   **133**

about to enter the tree. "Pip, pip, cheerio and I will see you again one day, I'm sure of it."

The children thanked him again for his hospitality as they stepped into the tree.

In what seemed like only a moment, Bobby awoke in her bed on another beautiful, sunny day, fully clothed and with the backpack on her back. I just can't work this out, she thought to herself. It's like I've had a dream but can't remember it … if only I could remember it. She sat up and rubbed her eyes. After a while she took off the backpack and looked inside. Yes, that's right, a crystal ball, and there are Anzac biscuits, a bottle of water and newspaper articles. That's right, she thought to herself: there's a great mystery and I have to solve it. Have I solved it yet? There was a boy too — what was his name? She reached into her jeans pocket — she wasn't sure why. Out came a neatly folded letter with her name on it.

Hello Bobby

This is the Professor Lambert and I know you don't remember me but I wrote this letter to jog your memory. Good grief, what an adventure you've had. Do you remember now that once you go back through the mists your brain completely forgets everything that it has experienced? It's part of the magic of this island. It's called self-preservation.

Anyhow, I know this will sound incredible to say

Linda Maree Malcolm

the least but can you bring yourself to remember my most esteemed colleague Sebastian the monkey and all of the natives living here on this island paradise?

Do you remember Ina and Henry who came here with six other stowaways and their dreadful experience in what they referred to as the workhouse? And what about the evil Oracle? You must by now remember David Game who, as fate would have it, is not only your very close friend but also a cousin of yours, of sorts. Do you remember being here with him, dancing by the bonfire on the beach and then the next day our resident Oracle sent you home together through the giant tree, back through the mists and back through time, as it were?

Anyway, my dear, we will be meeting again one day, I'm sure of it and in the meantime keep well and say hello to David for me.

Yours sincerely,
Professor Lambert,

P.S. I told David in his letter to call in and check on you so you can be expecting a knock on the door sometime soon.

Bobby sat blinking and turned the letter over and over as if to glean some kind of other clue as to who Professor Lambert even was. I must be dreaming, she thought to herself. I can't believe this. How on earth did this letter come to be in my pocket? Where did it come from? And yet the things it spoke of did seem familiar to her, like some kind of distant dream. She slowly became aware of the fact that this was the truth.

"Bobby, Bobby," Daphne was calling her name up the stairs. Bobby jumped out of her bed and ran down to the landing where her mother was standing. Never before had she been so completely happy to see her mother. It felt as if she hadn't seen her mother for a very long time. She bound into her mother's arms and hugged her tightly.

"I love you, Mum," she said and suddenly realised that this was something she hadn't said in a long time.

"I love you too, Bob-Bob," Daphne replied but then she held Bobby back by her shoulders and looked at her and asked, "Hey, what's going on? You look different. Are you okay and how come you're dressed already? Are you off to somewhere already?"

"Oh, no I'm fine; it's just such a beautiful day and I thought I might try and spend some time outdoors today."

"Okay, but first come and have some breakfast with me, will you?" her mother insisted.

"You know Bobby, it was strange last night. You went out and then I must have fallen asleep on the couch because I don't remember you coming home and then I woke up this morning still on the couch." Daphne looked at her, puzzled.

Linda Maree Malcolm

"Really," Bobby answered, avoiding eye contact. How she wished she could tell her mother about the crystal ball and the strange letter in her pocket but something told her that Daphne would not be approving of ... well, Bobby couldn't even work out what the mystery was anyway. Then there was a knock on the front door and David Game was standing on her step, just like the letter had said. Now she remembered him of course.

"I'm going out with my homeschool buddy, Daphne," she shouted from the door.

"Oh, okay then, see you later," came her mother's reply and Bobby and David walked off up the street together.

"Bobby, the most peculiar thing has happened," David started to say.

"I know. It happened to me too. Did you get the letter, David?" she asked and she reached into her pocket and pulled out the letter by Professor Lambert.

"Yes, what do you make of it?"

"It's too incredible to be true," said Bobby

"I know and yet what other explanation is there? Apparently we travelled through a wormhole or something, through time and to a parallel dimension and met Professor Lambert and all of the others. And apparently you and I are cousins. That's the part I can't believe." They stared at one another in disbelief and then they both started to laugh with the shock of it.

"David," Bobby stopped walking and looked at David seriously, "I don't actually remember anything about any of that and yet somehow in here," she pointed to her heart, "I know it to be the truth. There's no other way to explain these letters, is there?"

"I know, I know," he agreed, "it *must* have happened." They arrived at the milk bar and again ordered their milk shakes and went to sit in the window booth. They each sat silently, sipping on their straws and trying to absorb all of the information.

"Anyway, regardless of all of that, one thing's for sure," Bobby said turning to David. "I'm really glad that I have a cousin now. I can't tell you how many times I've wished for a cousin all through my life ..." Bobby stopped. She had a vague feeling of deja vu, as if maybe she had said this before.

"Yes, and I can't tell you how many times I've wished for a sister. It's all men in my house except for my mum of course. We all go a bit crazy when there's a female around because we're just not used to it." Bobby suppressed a smile as she knew this about David already. David continued, "Of course, it would have been good if ... oh never mind."

"What? It would be good if what?" Bobby tried to get to the bottom of what it was he was trying to say.

"Never mind. It's just a silly thing. So, what do you think we should tell people?"

"I don't know," she answered. "I don't think anyone would believe us anyway, do you?"

"Yes, that's the problem. And not only that but if it

leaked out to the authorities and government officials, the next thing you know our beautiful island paradise will be overrun with all kinds of people who are investigating and they'll ruin the serenity of the place and then they'll want to take a look at your mother's crystal ball ... and good heavens, Bobby, I just realised this could be disastrous if it gets into the hands of the wrong people. It could cause all kinds of problems for the past, the present and the future. We could have all time dimensions and places overrun with people and creatures from other time dimensions and places. You know, it's just occurred to me that even if someone did find out back in 1930 about the Oracle in the Mist of course it would have to be kept top secret. Maybe that's why all of this has been covered up so well ..."

Bobby noticed he had that pensive look on his face again.

"Well," she said at last, "if it's our little secret then there's nothing stopping us from going back whenever we want, is there? We can make the island like our second home. The perfect holiday destination."

"You think it's going to always be there though with that evil Oracle lurking around? What if she carries out her threat?"

"Well, we can't let her, can we? Surely you agree with me now David. We have to go back and do what we can to save what our grandparents created. Don't you think?"

"You make it sound so appealing. No, I'm not interested.

No more adventures for me. I think I've had just about all of the adventures I can handle and besides, pretty soon I'll be off to boarding school," David said, somewhat sadly.

"But come on David," Bobby persisted because she knew by now that David sometimes said no when he actually meant yes and because she also knew that she was prone to getting her own way with him. "Aren't you curious about everything else to do with our ancestors?"

"Such as?" David asked.

"Such as, how did things turn out for Ina and Henry once they returned to here? How did they get over the devastation of losing their son? You know, we could use the ball to go back to Ina and Henry's teenage years so that we could somehow introduce them to one another." Bobby was starting to feel excited just at the thought of doing that for her grandmother and also because another adventure was waiting just around the corner for her.

"You can't be serious, Bobby. There is no way I would do that, not in a million years. That's called meddling and who knows what sort of havoc would be created by messing about with time and lives like that?" David was adamant. "Besides, things must have turned out okay because your grandmother went ahead and married another man and then had your mother. And even then, I don't think you're able to just use the ball to go to any old place. We would need the voice of the Oracle to bring us through the mists, remember?" Both Bobby and David

Linda Maree Malcolm

could now clearly remember all of the details of their adventure.

"There must be a way though. I am an Oracle too, remember. I'm sure I could make it work somehow. And aren't you curious to know what became of your grandfather, David? We have the power to find the answers to our questions now. Aren't you even just a little interested?" Bobby persisted.

"The way you used that word 'power' just now really frightens me Bobby. Don't you care if you get hurt? I really mean it, Bobby. This isn't something you should muck around with. And don't you go pulling any stunts while I'm away at boarding school either, will you? Promise?"

Bobby smiled. She didn't answer him because she thought it better not to make a promise that she didn't plan on keeping. She knew she would use the ball again, with or without him, it was just a question of when. And as she slurped the chocolate soya milk noisily from the bottom of the glass, she shivered inside at the thought of what her next adventure would be and where it would take her.